FRIGHT TIME

3 Spine-tingling Tales for Young Readers

- DON'T BREATHE
- OVERNIGHT-MARE
- IT'S IN THE ATTIC

BARONET
B·O·O·K·S

Baronet Books, New York, New York

DON'T BREATHE

by Roy Nemerson

1

I let out a gasp.

Suddenly everyone was staring at me. "What was that?" the coach asked, and he looked really scared.

I tried to say something. But all I could do was gasp again.

"He has asthma," a classmate called out. "He needs his inhalator. Fast!"

"His inhalator!" yelled the coach. "Where is it?"

I couldn't answer. I was gasping every two or three seconds now. I dropped to my knees, and pointed toward the locker room area.

FRIGHT TIME

"It must be in his locker!" one of the kids called out. "We'll get it!" Two of the boys dashed off toward the locker area as the other kids all gathered around.

"Okay, give him space, give him air!" the coach said.

Air! There was plenty of air. The problem was getting it into my lungs. Especially after just having done twenty push ups. Ever since I was three years old I had been having attacks of asthma.

The attacks could be controlled by my breath-inhalator. It was a little plastic device that I placed into my mouth. I'd press down on it, and it would open up the passages and let me breathe normally again.

The boys had returned with my inhalator. Everyone watched as I pressed on the button and breathed in the misty spray. In two or three seconds I began to breathe normally again. My wheezing stopped.

"I'm okay, thanks," I said, as I stood up. Everyone was staring at me like they had seen a ghost.

"Sorry if I scared you," I said. "It looks and sounds a lot worse than it really is. I'm fine."

"What do you mean?" the coach said, trying to stay calm. "If we couldn't get your inhalator, you might have passed out, or worse!"

"I never travel anywhere without it," I said. "So it's never a problem."

The coach looked at me, and nodded. "You've got courage, Ricky. And I admire your spirit. But health and safety come before everything else. And no one told me I was getting a gym student who had asthma. You shouldn't have been doing those push-ups."

I felt my cheeks turning red again, but this time with anger and frustration. People were always treating me like I was weak or something. But I wasn't! I had the asthma under control.

"Really, it was nothing," I said. "You saw, I did the twenty push ups and some of the other kids couldn't. And they don't have asthma."

"Sorry, son," said the coach, shaking his head. "We can't take any chances. From now on, no more strenuous activity for you without approval or permission from the school doctor."

"It's not fair!" I said to my mother, who was busy getting dinner.

"They're just doing what they think's best for you, Ricky. You can still play baseball and tennis and the other sports. You just have to take it easy on the pushups and things like that."

"I thought it'd be different in junior high," I said. "That they wouldn't treat me like a baby once I was in the seventh grade."

"They're not," she said. "They just want to be careful. The doctors say your condition's better, but there's no point taking chances now."

"It's no big deal!" I pleaded. "I'm getting fewer attacks, I've always got my inhalator with me, the whole thing's over in a few seconds!"

"Ricky, don't get yourself all worked up," Mom said, frowning at me. "That's a good way to give yourself another attack."

It just wasn't fair, I thought, as I stared glumly out the kitchen window. A squirrel was busy burying a nut in the ground in our backyard. Winters came early in this part of New England, and the animals knew when it was time to prepare. I sighed. It looked like it was going to be a long winter for me, too.

"Pack your bags, family!" boomed out a voice behind me.

I whirled around. Mom and I both stared at Dad, who was standing in the kitchen doorway. He was smiling broadly.

"We're moving to Florida!"

2

Dad was a research chemist with Dalton Industries. We'd lived just north of Boston all my life, where Dalton had a major laboratory and research center.

"Are you being transferred by Dalton?" Mom asked. She was as amazed as I was.

"Better than that!" Dad beamed. "I've accepted an offer from Keyser Chemicals. They're a big up-and-coming company, and I'll be working on some exciting new projects."

"Florida," I said. "Wow! No more winter." The cold New England winters weren't that good for my asthma. Just thinking of the warmth of Florida made my lungs feel stronger already.

"When are we moving?" Mom asked, still a little dazed.

"Tomorrow," Dad said.

"Tomorrow!" Mom exclaimed.

"Yep," Dad said, smiling. "I start working at Keyser Chemicals the following day."

Mom stared at him. "But we have to find a place to live. And Ricky's schooling. And we have to sell this house."

Dad put up a hand. "It's all taken care of. Keyser provides for all of that for its employees. There's nothing to worry about. We're on the noon flight tomorrow."

The next twenty-four hours were a whirlwind. There was packing to be done. Throwing out things we wouldn't need. Calling friends and relatives to tell them about the move.

I thought about what it would mean for me. I'd liked the town where I'd lived all my life. But maybe because of the asthma I'd never felt one hundred per cent accepted. I was friendly with a lot of kids, but I had no real best friend. Maybe in a new town, with new kids, it would be different. I was ready for an exciting new life!

The excitement started with the flight down to Florida. It was the first time I'd ever been on a plane!

"This is great, Dad!" I exclaimed.

Mom tapped me on the knee. "Yes, Ricky, but listen to the flight attendant now."

Mom was right. The head attendant was standing in the front of the cabin and demonstrating emergency procedures. He pointed to the emergency exits. He held up a life preserver.

Don't Breathe

And then he held an emergency oxygen mask up to cover his mouth and nose. He said if there was an emergency, a mask would drop right in front of you and you could breathe through it. I realized how much the mask reminded me of my asthma inhalator.

Fortunately, our flight was smooth and no emergency equipment was needed.

Soon we were standing in the terminal, our bags beside us. "What's next, Dad?" I asked.

"Someone's supposed to pick us up," Dad replied, glancing at his watch.

"Doctor Daniels?" asked a young man, approaching us.

"Yes," Dad replied. Dad had a doctoral degree in chemistry, and so people often called him doctor out of respect.

"My name is Jeffrey, and I'll be taking you and your family to Keyserville, sir."

Jeffrey was in his twenties. He had short blond hair, dark eyes, and a serious face. He wore slacks and a shirt with a Keyser Chemicals logo on the front pocket.

We picked up our bags and followed Jeffrey out to a private hangar section. Jeffrey loaded our bags into the rear of a small plane that had the Keyser logo across its side. Then we boarded the plane.

Mom and Dad got in the back seats and I sat up front with Jeffrey. I couldn't believe it. I was about to have the second flight of my life, and this one in a neat little one-engine plane.

"How long is the flight to Keyserville?" Dad asked.

"About twenty minutes, doctor." Jeffrey started up the engine, and in minutes we were cleared for take-off and on our way.

As we climbed, I looked over at Jeffrey. "Does this plane have emergency masks like the jet we came down on?" I asked.

"Yes," Jeffrey replied. "They're located above each seat. It's a Federal law."

We quickly flew inland, and as I looked down I saw nothing but swampy green wetlands.

"That must be the Everglades!" I said.

"Yes," Jeffrey replied. But that's all he said. In fact, Jeffrey would have said nothing at all if you didn't ask him a question. Maybe he was shy.

I didn't feel like talking much anyway. The view of Everglades National Park had me speechless. It seemed to go on forever. It was unlike anything I'd ever seen before. I knew from school that the Everglades had a lot of dangerous animal life, like alligators and snakes. And that quicksand and other deadly menaces were down there, too.

It seemed like only moments had passed when Jeffrey said, "Okay, prepare for landing, keep your seat belts fastened until the plane has come to a complete stop."

We were landing? Where? And then suddenly I saw it. Carved out on the edge of a river bank in the swamp, was an entire community. As the plane descended, we passed over rows of houses and suburban streets. I saw a school and a shopping mall. In the center of the community, as we approached rapidly and got lower and lower, was a huge, amazing-looking group of buildings. The buildings were many stories tall and some had giant smokestacks.

"What's that?" I asked, as blue and yellow smoke puffed out of one of the stacks.

"That," Jeffrey said, "is the main research and manufacturing center of Keyser Chemicals. That's where your dad's going to work." I noticed the Keyser Chemicals name and logo was on every building in sight.

And then just beyond the complex a landing strip came into view. The plane headed down. Within moments we were touching down. We pulled up to a main gate and Jeffrey turned off the engine.

"Welcome to Keyserville," Jeffrey said, unbuckling his seat belt.

"I guess that means we're home," Dad said.

Suddenly Jeffrey turned around. His mouth was twisted. He rocked from side to side, like he was having a seizure.

"Get out!" he shouted, the veins in his neck bulging. His eyes had a yellow glow to them. "Out of Keyserville. While you still can!"

3

We watched in shocked silence as Jeffrey dropped to the ground. He let out a cry and lay there, not moving.

"We have to do something!" Mom yelled. "Get help, fast!"

"We'll handle it," said a voice from behind us. A small van with the words Keyserville Security across its hood had pulled to a halt. Several men jumped out and immediately placed Jeffrey, who was groaning in pain, on a stretcher. Then they placed a mask over his face. The mask was attached to a gas pump. They turned knobs on the pump. I heard a whooshing sound, as first a yellow and then a blue gas entered the mask area around Jeffrey's mouth and nose.

Jeffrey was trying to struggle, but in moments his body went limp. Then the men loaded him into the van and drove off.

The man who had spoken to us stayed. He smiled and held out his hand. "Doctor Daniels? I'm Robert Lawrence. Sorry about that little problem there, but welcome to Keyserville, to you and your family."

Dad shook Mr. Lawrence's hand. "What was that all about?" Dad asked, speaking for Mom and me as well.

"Oh, sometimes these young people put too much pressure on themselves. Jeffrey's a good kid, he'll be fine, don't you worry. Come along with me, we'll get you settled."

We followed Mr. Lawrence toward a car parked near the landing strip. We loaded our bags into the trunk, and got in. Mr. Lawrence got behind the wheel, and we drove off.

Except for the warm air and sun, you wouldn't know you were in Florida, let alone right on the Everglades. Keyserville had been built to look like any typical American suburb.

"Keyser Chemicals has created a completely self-contained community. Everyone in Keyserville works for the company. We've provided a perfect suburban setting, complete with homes, schools, hospitals, ball fields, shopping malls, everything," Mr. Lawrence said, as we drove past the sights.

"You seem to have your own police force as well," Mom noted, looking out the car window. On almost every corner there was a uniformed officer, like the ones who had come to take Jeffrey away. "Is that because there's a lot of crime?"

"Oh no!" Mr. Lawrence roared with laughter. "In fact, just the opposite. We have very little crime in Keyserville."

"Then why all the police?" Mom asked.

For the first time the smile seemed to harden on Mr. Lawrence's face. "You can never have too much security, Mrs. Daniels." And there was no more conversation until we pulled up to our new home.

The house was painted white, with a black

roof. It had a broad driveway. All the other houses on the street looked just like ours, only with different colors.

"Well, here we are," Mr. Lawrence said. "You must be tired, so you'll want to get settled in. Here's the key to your house. Everything should be in order. A new car in the garage. Telephones. Cable TV. Kitchen appliances. Everything. Doctor Daniels, here's where you're to report to work," Mr. Lawrence said, handing Dad a card. "And if you need anything, call me at the number on the card."

"Thank you, Mr. Lawrence," Dad said, "and we hope things work out for that pilot."

"Oh, don't you worry about young Jeffrey," Mr. Lawrence said, "he'll be taken care of just fine. Welcome to Keyserville, folks. You're never going to want to leave." His voice was pleasant enough. But there was something about it and about him that gave me a slight chill. I let out a little wheeze. Mom and Dad both looked at me, a bit concerned.

"You okay, Ricky?" Dad asked.

"Yes, Dad, I'm fine," I said, not liking to be babied like that.

"Brought a little cold with you from up

north?" Mr. Lawrence asked, smiling at me.

Before either of my parents could say anything, I said, "Yes, but it's just a little sniffle. Nothing much."

"Well, you're in Keyserville, Florida now, son," Mr. Lawrence said. "No more colds. And no more cold." Mr. Lawrence smiled and winked at me. Then with a nod, he drove off.

We started toward the house with our bags and cases. "Nobody has to know about the asthma," I said. "It's real warm and mild down here, and I may never get another attack."

"You almost had one just now," Mom said, as we approached the front door.

"That was nothing," I said. "Just clearing my throat."

"Oh sure," Dad said. "And that young pilot was just having an attack of nerves."

"What do you think was wrong with him, dear?" Mom asked Dad. "What he said to us was frightening."

"And did you see his eyes?" I added. "They turned from blue to yellow."

"Well, I'm not a medical doctor," Dad said, putting the key in the front door. "But my guess was that young man was having a chemical reaction of some kind. I've seen it happen in laboratory mice. It's not pleasant."

"It certainly wasn't," Mom agreed. "Why was he telling us to get away from here? What could that have meant?"

Dad had opened the front door and I stepped inside. And what I saw knocked all thoughts of the pilot or anything else clear out of my head. The lights had come on automatically. The downstairs living room was filled with TV screens, monitors, VCRs, and neat looking furniture.

"Wow!" I said, and wondered how great my bedroom would be. As my parents looked around, staring at everything, I dashed up the stairs toward the bedroom area. There was a large bedroom on the right, obviously for my parents. There was a small room to the left. The door was partially closed. I pushed it open and entered. This had to be my room.

"My new home!" I announced. And I took a step back and let out a gasp.

My eyes were drawn toward the bed. The bed had a white blanket covering it. And lying on the blanket was a small blue parakeet. "Hey, little guy," I said, approaching softly. "Who are you? How'd you get in here?"

I reached the bed and bent down to get a better look at the little bird. It was dead.

4

I brought the little blue bird downstairs. My parents were surprised when I showed it to them.

"It was lying on the bed in your room?" Mom asked.

"Yes," I replied. "What do you think it was doing there? Did it get in somehow? Did someone leave it behind? And how did it die? Nothing seems broken or anything," I said, staring at it, feeling sorry for the little thing.

"We'll probably never know, dear," Mom said. "Why don't you take it outside and place it beneath the soil near one of the bushes?"

I did as Mom suggested. I went downstairs and out the front door. As I was placing the small bird in the soil, I suddenly sensed someone standing behind me. I turned around.

A girl about my age, with long red hair, freckles, and blue eyes, was staring down at the ground. When she saw what I was doing she let out a shriek.

"Oh no!" she shrieked. "That's the Websters' bird. The experiments are getting worse! Where is this all going to end?" She was practically in tears.

"Who are you?" I asked, as the girl continued to tremble. "What's going on?"

"I'm sorry," she said, wiping her cheeks. She was getting herself under control. "It's just been so weird. I'm scared. Really scared."

"Scared of what?"

"I'm Lisa White, we live across the street," she said, pointing to the yellow house across the way.

"I'm Ricky Daniels," I said. "We just moved in today. My dad's going to work at Keyser as a chemist. What are you scared of, Lisa?"

Lisa's eyes widened in terror. "Your dad's going to be a chemist at Keyser? Tell him not to go, Ricky. Don't let him do it. They're doing awful things there."

Before either of us could say could say another word, a woman leaned out of the front door of Lisa's house. She had the exact same red hair color as Lisa's. "Lisa, let's go, it's getting late!"

she called over. She was speaking to Lisa, but I noticed she was also looking at me.

"That's my mom," Lisa said. "I have to go."

There was so much more I wanted to ask her. "What grade are you in?" I asked quickly, as she turned to leave.

"Seventh," she replied.

"Me, too," I said. "Maybe I'll see you tomorrow at school."

"Lisa! I said now!" her mother called out, her voice rising.

"You better go, she sounds a little angry," I said.

"She was never like that. Only since we moved here and she started working at the labs," Lisa said, her eyes filled with concern. Suddenly she looked sharply at me. "Ricky, look, tonight there's a Keyser Kids meeting."

"Keyser Kids? What's that?" I asked.

"Every boy and girl in the community has to attend the weekly meetings. Tonight it's for the kids in our age group. It's held in the school assembly room, at seven p.m. They'll expect you to be there."

"Lisa!" her mother nearly shouted.

"Coming, Mother," Lisa called back. She

looked down at where I'd placed the little bird, then back at me. "Seven o'clock, Ricky," she said, and her voice was barely a whisper. Then she turned and dashed off toward her house. I watched as her mother said something to her, and then looked over at me. Lisa was right; her mother did not look happy at all.

That evening, after dinner, Dad drove me down to the school in our new car.

"Call me when the meeting's over and I'll come pick you up," he said, as we pulled up in front of the school.

"Okay, Dad," I said. I hadn't told my parents anything that Lisa had said. I didn't want to scare them, in case Lisa was making things up or imagining them. She had seemed very sincere and honest, but I thought I should wait and see a few things around here for myself.

I got out, Dad drove off, and I headed for the school entrance. Large, bold letters spelled out KEYSER JUNIOR HIGH above the massive doors. Lots of other kids were filing in, and I followed the flow.

The kids were all about my age, and I noticed how orderly and well-behaved everyone was.

"Hi, my name's Ricky Daniels," I said to a boy

walking next to me, "What's your's?" The boy glanced at me, said nothing, and continued walking on.

As I looked around I realized there was no joking, no talking, no smiles. It wasn't what I was used to back home, where there was always chatter in the hallways between classes. I looked around for Lisa but couldn't find her. Maybe I'd see her in the meeting room.

I followed the group into a large room. In a matter of minutes we were all seated at desks facing the front of the room. Above the green blackboard was a banner with the Keyser logo. You couldn't go more than a few steps without seeing the name "Keyser" around here.

The room had shiny white gleaming walls. I felt like I was in a creepy sci-fi movie. I looked around and noticed that Lisa had slipped into a nearby desk.

"Hi," I started to say. She immediatley cut me off by shaking her head "no" and putting a finger up to her lips. I realized I'd better keep quiet.

"Hello, children," came a voice from the front.

"Hello, Mr. Lawrence!" everyone replied together. I was startled. I looked up front. Mr. Lawrence, the man who had met us at the airport, was now standing in front of the class. He had on a jacket with the word "Keyser" spelled out across the front.

"First, I want to give you this week's instructions. You are to turn in the names of any student, parent, or teacher who you think is being disloyal to Keyserville. Even if it's your own parents, teachers, brothers, or sisters. Is that clear?"

"Yes, Mr. Lawrence!" everyone shouted as one.

I looked on in shock. What was going on here?

"That boy didn't say yes!" a girl behind me suddenly called out. The entire classroom let out a shocked gasp. Everyone turned and stared. And I realized they were staring at me!

5

I suddenly felt frightened. All the faces staring at me were filled with hatred. And my breathing was starting to feel funny.

"It's okay, children," Mr. Lawrence said, smiling that thin smile again. "That's your newest classmate, Ricky Daniels. He and his family just arrived in Keyserville today. Ricky doesn't know how to behave yet. But he'll soon learn."

While Mr. Lawrence was talking I slipped my hand into my pants pocket and pulled out my inhalator. I hid it in my hand as I raised it into my mouth, and quickly hit the button. The mist entered my throat and lungs, and instantly my breathing returned to normal. I slipped the inhalator back into my pocket.

"In fact, this is a perfect time for Ricky to receive his first lesson. Don't you agree, children?"

"Yes, Mr. Lawrence!" everyone responded. I glanced over at Lisa. I noticed she was answering with everyone else, but she seemed different. The others were acting like robots. Lisa seemed to be just going along. And she was looking at me with great concern on her face.

"Ricky, you'll find it's quite easy, really. Just sit back in your seat and relax. Think about how happy you are to be in Keyserville. How your life is never going to be the same again. How you're never going to want to leave Keyserville. Aren't you feeling better already, Ricky?" Mr. Lawrence asked.

I didn't know what to say. I glanced around the room. All the kids, including Lisa, were sitting back in their seats, their eyes half-closed. And then I noticed the gas.

It was coming in silently through large vents in the side of the room. It was a pale blue, and it filled the room, giving the air a slightly blue tint. I breathed in. It had no smell at all. And I felt no effect from it. Nothing was happening to me, it seemed.

"Ricky!" Mr. Lawrence called out. I snapped my head to look at him.

"I asked you a question. Don't you suddenly feel better? Don't you suddenly feel like Keyserville is the most important thing in your life? More important than your friends, your family, even your own life?"

Was this man insane? I felt I had to say the right thing right now, to say what he wanted to hear, otherwise I might be putting myself in great danger. "Uh, yes, Mr. Lawrence, I really like it here," I said, hesitating a little.

Mr. Lawrence stared at me. He seemed a little uncertain. Like he wasn't sure how to take my answer. I noticed the gas had stopped being piped into the room. Around me the kids seemed to come out of their trances and sit up in their seats.

"Okay, children, that's all for tonight," Mr. Lawrence said. "You have your instructions for this week. I will see you all next week at the same time. Dismissed!"

All together, everyone stood at the same moment, and they began filing out of the room the same way they had entered. Quietly, in perfect order. Like a small army. A brainwashed army.

As I walked out, trying to be like the others, I noticed Mr. Lawrence staring at me. He was watching me very carefully.

As soon as I got to the main lobby area I looked around for Lisa. She was a little way up ahead. I pushed past several kids to get to her. They glared at me like I had just done something horrible.

I reached Lisa. "Hey, what exactly is the deal around here?" I asked.

"Sshh!" she said, looking around nervously. "Not in the school halls," she whispered. "Talking isn't allowed. Wait until we get outside. And you must not walk out of line. It's not permitted."

"Not permitted? What is this, a school or a prison?" I asked.

Lisa didn't talk to me until we were outside. We walked down the path leading away from the school, toward the sidewalk, where we could finally speak.

"Did you realize what was happening back

there?" I asked. "Do you know that gas was being pumped into that room?"

"Of course I knew it," Lisa said. "They do it every week. It's how they keep everyone under control."

"You seem different," I said. "You don't seem 'controlled'."

"I know," Lisa replied. "And neither do you. I can't believe it. The gas didn't affect you?"

"No, nothing," I said. "But it seemed to make everyone else into zombies."

"It's been that way ever since we came here two months ago," Lisa said. "We arrived on a Saturday, and by Sunday morning my parents were both acting so different, so strangely. They didn't smile or laugh or seem to really care about me. My mother spends practically all her time at the Keyser research lab, and won't tell us what she's working on. My dad is an architect and the only thing he focuses on is drawing up plans for an even bigger, newer research plant to develop more chemicals and gases."

"This is creepy," I said. I told Lisa about the strange behavior of Jeffrey, our plane pilot.

"That's not so strange," Lisa replied. "I don't know what causes it, but I've seen it happen to other people around here. They suddenly seem to freak out. Then they get carried off for treatment, and you never see them again. It's frightening. It's what happened to the Websters, the people who lived in your house before you moved in there."

"And what about their little bird?"

"Whatever happened to them, it obviously killed their bird." Lisa paused. "They were nice people. He was a nice little bird."

We had reached a street crossing. It was now totally dark. I glanced across the way. Straight ahead, in the center of Keyserville, was the huge chemical research complex. At night it was even scarier looking. It was all lit up, and glowing yellow and blue.

"Whatever's going on around here," Lisa said, "the answer is in that place." And she nodded toward the chemical works.

"Maybe we should talk to a police officer," I said. "They seem to have plenty of them around here."

Lisa laughed. "You don't understand. *Everybody* is weird here. Until I saw you today, I thought I was the only one left who hadn't been changed. The police aren't going to help. They're like everyone else."

"You mean everyone arrives here normal, but then suddenly changes? And it's got something to do with this gas business?" I asked.

"Every single one," Lisa said. "Until now." She stared at me.

"I don't know why we're different, but my guess is by the time you get home, your parents will be just like mine. Changed."

I felt a chill go up my spine. "Don't be crazy!" I said. "Nothing's going to happen to my mom and dad."

"I'm sorry, Ricky," Lisa said, "but I wouldn't count on that."

Just then a car came racing up the street, and caught me and Lisa in its headlights, blinding us for a moment.

"Ricky!" a voice called out. I didn't recognize the voice. It sounded cold and unfriendly.

"Ricky Daniels!" the voice boomed out again. It was coming from the driver's side of the car. It was a man, but I did not know who it was.

I shielded my eyes with my hand. "Yes?" I said. "Who is it?"

Who was calling out my name like that?

"Come over here," the voice called out. I walked around to the driver's side.

"I need to talk to you," the man said, from behind the wheel. His front window was down.

I glanced inside to see who it was who had called out my name. I staggered back in shock. Sitting behind the wheel was my father!

"It's important," he said in a voice I had never heard before. And his eyes had a faint yellow glow.

"Dad! Are you all right?" I gasped.

"Of course," he said, and smiled the same kind of thin smile I had seen before. The way Mr. Lawrence smiled!

"What are you doing out here?" I asked. "I was going to call you to come pick me up."

"A change in plans. I've been summoned to the labs, they want me to start work tonight."

"Tonight!" I said. "But we just arrived today. What's the rush?"

"The rush, young man," Dad said, cutting me

off, "is the protection and well-being of Keyserville. Nothing comes ahead of that. Nothing! Do you understand?"

Dad had never talked to me, or anyone else, like that. It was like someone else was telling him what to say. I felt like screaming, crying, hitting something or somebody. Lisa put a hand on my elbow.

"How should I get home then, Dad?" I asked, my voice a little unsteady.

"How should I know!" Dad thundered. "That's your problem. I have work to do. Good night!" And with that, Dad stepped on the gas, and the car roared off toward the eerie, huge chemical plant in the distance.

"It's okay," Lisa said. "There's a bus that stops right near our homes."

I followed Lisa in stunned silence. She didn't say anything, but I could tell she was watching me closely. The bus came, we got aboard, and headed home.

We sat in the back of the bus. Finally Lisa spoke. "It's really tough, I know," she said. "But remember, that wasn't your dad talking. It was something he has no control over, making him act that way."

"I suppose you're right," I said. "But it doesn't make it any easier. Lisa, we have to do something. We can't just let things go on like this!"

Several passengers turned and stared at me and Lisa. "Sshh," Lisa said, squeezing my arm. "Remember," she said, speaking very low, "everyone here is under control. You have to be careful. If anyone suspects we're being different, or disloyal, we could find ourselves in big trouble. And then we won't be able to help anyone."

I had to agree. She was right. The bus dropped us off, and we stood on the sidewalk in front of our homes.

"Try to act like you're one of them," Lisa said. "That way no one will become suspicious, and maybe we'll be able to think of something."

"I think your idea is right," I said. "We're going to have to get into the chemical plant and find out what's going on. And maybe do something to stop it."

"Yes," Lisa said, "the only problem is you need ID clearance to get in, and we don't have any. My mother does and your father does, but we don't."

"What kind of clearance?" I asked.

"They issue them plastic ID cards. It's the only way you can get in," she replied.

I thought for a moment. "What time does your mom go to the plant tomorrow?" I asked.

"Tomorrow's actually her one day off the whole month," Lisa said.

"Great!" I responded. "Do you know where she keeps her ID card?"

Lisa stared at me. She understood what I was thinking. "If I take her card to use it to get us into the plant and we get caught," Lisa said, "we may never get out alive."

"I hear you," I said, feeling the fear rise in my throat. "But we can't think about that. We can only think about what we have to do."

Lisa looked at me and smiled. "When you put it like that, I have to agree," she said. "And it sure feels good to have a friend," she added.

"For me, too," I said.

"Then here's what I'll do," Lisa said. "I'll take the card from my mother's bag tonight, and bring it to school with me tomorrow. Then you meet me outside right after school, and we'll go from there."

"I'm willing to if you are," I said. "You know, most of my life people have treated me differently, like a baby at times," I admitted to her.

"Why's that?" Lisa asked.

"Oh, it's really stupid. I have a minor asthma condition. But people make a big deal out of it."

"Me, too!" Lisa said.

"You have asthma!" I said, surprised.

"No, I have a minor form of diabetes. It's the medical name for low blood sugar. I have to give myself a little injection of insulin every morning, and then I'm fine. But people treat me sometimes as if I might break like a doll, and that's not so at all."

"Well, how do you like that? Looks like the two 'sick kids' are going to have to be the ones to get everyone healthy this time." I smiled at my new friend. "Partners?" I asked.

"Partners," she replied. We shook hands, and then Lisa headed for her house and I headed for mine.

When I entered the living room, Mom was standing with her back to me. She was talking on the telephone.

"Yes, Mr. Lawrence. Ricky's had asthma since he was a little boy. He uses an inhalator. That's right," Mom said into the phone. She paused as she listened to whatever Mr. Lawrence was saying. "Of course we won't tell him what we're doing. You have my word. My husband has already gone off to begin his research, and my instructions are to destroy all of Ricky's inhalators. Those are my orders, and I will follow them."

7

I gasped and leaned back against the wall, as Mom hung up the phone and headed upstairs. She was under their control, just like Dad! And like Lisa's mom. And like Jeffrey the pilot had been. Like the kids at the meeting. And like everyone else in Keyserville apparently was. Except me. And Lisa.

I noticed there was a faint blue mist in the air. I looked up. There was a wall vent high up in the ceiling. The gas must have come from out of there. So that's how they did it! If they didn't get you at school they got you at home. Or maybe at your job. Or maybe at the mall, or in your car. They could be pumping the gas in from anyplace. But why? And who was behind this? Was Mr. Lawrence in charge? He was obviously involved, but he didn't have the look of someone who was in charge.

I had to think quickly. Mr. Lawrence found

out I had asthma, and that was apparently important. I didn't know why, but it could have been the reason Dad was called to report to work in the middle of his first night in town.

Suddenly I heard noises upstairs, the sound of glass or plastic breaking. Mom was destroying my supply of inhalators! The one I had on me now was my last one! And it probably only had a few doses left in it.

It couldn't wait until tomorrow. We had to get into the Keyser chemical plant now. Tonight!

I slipped quietly out of the house and dashed across the darkened street. The lights were on in Lisa's house. The car was in the driveway so her parents were home. How could I get Lisa out, and bring her mother's ID card with her, and not raise her parents' suspicions? I decided to take the risk.

I rang the front doorbell. A moment later Lisa's father opened the door.

"Yes?" he asked, looking at me with a blank stare. There seemed to be a yellow tint in his eyes.

"Mr. White, my name's Ricky Daniels, my family moved in across the street today," I said. I tried to get that "controlled" sound into my voice, so Lisa's dad wouldn't become suspicious of me.

"Yes?" he asked again. "What is it you want?"

"My parents have asked me to invite you and Mrs. White over for a cup of coffee. They'd like to get to meet you."

By this time Lisa's mother had come to the door and was standing next to Mr. White.

"What does the boy want?" Mrs. White said, looking at me sternly. Mr. White repeated what I had said.

"Oh," Mrs. White said. "Okay, that sounds all right."

"Oh fine," I said. "Right across, we're the white house. They said come over right now, coffee's just about ready."

Mrs. White turned and glanced up the stairs. "Lisa, we're going out for a little while. Be sure to finish your homework, and don't leave the house."

"Okay, Mother," Lisa replied from upstairs. Lisa's parents walked out the front door, and headed for our house. I fell back behind them. As soon as they started to cross the street, I turned back and rang Lisa's front door, keeping my finger on the buzzer.

A moment later Lisa appeared.

"What?" she started to say when she saw me, but I cut her off.

"Hurry, get your mother's ID card, then meet me down the road. I'll explain it all to you. We've only got a minute before your parents will be back, Lisa!"

Lisa turned and raced up the stairs. I turned and darted off down the street, out of the light. I looked across the way toward my house. Lisa's parents had reached our front door. They were talking to Mom, who was standing in the doorway. The Whites turned and pointed toward their house. It was obvious that their conversation was a confusing one.

And a moment later the Whites said good-bye to Mom, turned, and headed back across the street toward their house. They were moving quickly, as they obviously suspected something.

"Lisa, hurry!" I almost yelled it out loud. But too late. Her parents were already at the front door and Lisa hadn't come out yet. Our plan wasn't going to work. Worse, Lisa and I would now be separated and isolated. Her parents would probably find her with the ID card in hand, and have her arrested, or worse. And my mom was probably already on the phone alerting the authorities that I was on the loose and should be brought in.

"Got it!" came a voice behind me. I nearly jumped out of my skin. I turned around. Lisa was standing next to me. And in the darkness I could see she was holding up a shiny ID card.

"How'd you pull that off?" I said. "I saw your parents go back in the front door, but you never came out."

"Not the front door," Lisa replied. "But out the back one. I thought it'd be safer."

"Good thinking," I said. We got on the first bus heading downtown. I quickly filled Lisa in on what I had overheard my mother saying to Mr. Lawrence on the phone. The bus was nearly empty, and we were sitting in the back, so no one could overhear us.

"It sounds to me like they're making a big deal out of your having asthma," said Lisa. "I wonder why."

"They always do," I said, with a shrug. "I wonder how they found out. I used my inhalator in the meeting room tonight. Maybe Mr. Lawrence saw me."

"Once they had your parents under control, they probably asked them a bunch of questions. They always do that. Your having asthma could have come up. And it set off an alarm bell somewhere."

"The somewhere being the chemical plant," I said. Lisa looked at me and nodded. For the next several minutes we rode in silence, as I stared out the bus window. We were passing some of the big malls, with shopping centers and movie theaters. There were people everywhere. Parents with their little children. Teenagers. Elderly people.

"It all looks so normal," I said. "You'd never suspect anything was wrong."

"Things aren't always the way they look," Lisa said. "Okay," she continued, rising, "here's our stop."

The bus had pulled up to the entrance area to the chemical complex. We got off the bus and it pulled away.

We looked up at the huge main building. "Have you ever been inside before?" I asked.

"No," said Lisa, looking up at the dark, large,

scary-looking building. The words "Keyser Chemicals" were in huge letters above us. Lisa's eyes seemed to be filled with fear. But then I realized at that moment mine probably were, too.

"Once we get inside, we have to act like everyone else," Lisa said. "We can't make anybody suspicious."

"All I want to do is see what my father is up to," I said. "Once I see that, we'll have a better idea of what we need to do next."

"There's the main entrance," Lisa said. There was a gate, with a uniformed armed guard standing duty. People were entering the complex by the gate. We watched as a man placed his ID card into a slot. Then something buzzed and the man entered through the opened gate. It snapped closed again.

"Okay," Lisa said softly. "Our turn." We walked up, trying to look and act as natural as possible. The guard gave us a hard look as Lisa inserted her mother's ID card into the slot. Nothing happened.

"What's wrong?" I whispered to Lisa.

"I don't know," she whispered back, trying to keep the panic out of her voice. "But it's not working. The gate won't open!"

Suddenly the guard was standing next to us. "Let me have that card," he said, his voice cold, his face stern. Something was wrong. I was about to tell Lisa to run for it, that we should split off in different directions, when the guard inserted the card into the slot. Instantly the gate door buzzed open.

"You inserted it the wrong way," he said. "You had it upside down." He held the card in his hand, looked at the name on it. "I haven't seen you here before. Karen White?"

"Yes," said Lisa, trying to act and look calm. "We're part of a new project," she said.

The guard hesitated. He stared at the card again, then back at us. "Why doesn't he have his own card?" he asked, nodding toward me.

"You're going to make us late for our appointment, sir," Lisa said, suddenly taking the card from the guard's hand. "You wouldn't want to be the cause of trouble, would you?"

"No, I wouldn't," the guard said, and before he could say another word Lisa grabbed my arm and we were through the gate and into the main lobby area.

"That was cool," I said. "I thought we might be finished before we even got started."

"I've noticed that being under the control of the gas affects the way people behave. They're good at taking orders, but their minds aren't so fast. It's like they're almost a little drugged."

"It was fast thinking on your part," I said.

"I owed it to us, partner," Lisa said. "It was pretty stupid of me, inserting the ID card upside down."

"That's over, we're inside now," I said, looking around. The lobby area was enormous. People moved about in all directions. Men and women. Some were dressed in chemists' lab coats, others in business suits.

But just like at the school, there was no talking, no feeling of human contact between the people. It gave me a chill to watch it. The people seemed like robots.

"There's a directory," Lisa said, pointing toward a rear wall. "Let's check it out. It should show where your father is located."

We headed for it. "My dad's in Project Research," I said, as we reached the directory and stared at it.

"Yes, there it is, Project Research, fourth floor!" Lisa said.

Just then an alarm siren rang out over the PA

system. A voice boomed out. "Attention! All Keyser employees! A boy and girl named Ricky Daniels and Lisa White are believed to be within the complex. They are both twelve years old. They are enemies of Keyser Chemicals. They must be found and brought to Keyser Command Control immediately!"

"Quick, through this door!" I shouted, grabbing Lisa by the arm and pushing her through a door marked "EXIT/STAIRCASE" before anyone could see us.

We dashed through the door, closing it behind us. We found ourselves on the landing of a service staircase.

"How did they find out about us so fast?" I asked, breathing slightly hard.

"My parents and your mom. They probably realized we'd tricked them into being together to get my parents out of my house. Mom probably checked all her things and found her ID card missing, so they realized we'd headed over here."

"Our own parents turned us in," I said, my breathing returning to normal.

"It's the gas. It controls them. Remember that, Ricky. They're being controlled. But we don't have time to worry about that now. The big question is do we try to get out of here or do we push on?"

"If we manage to get out, it won't help," I said. "They'll be looking for us everywhere. We're considered enemies of Keyserville now. As long as we're inside, we may as well push on and at least go down fighting."

"Okay," Lisa said. She looked up. "Let's see if these stairs lead to the fourth floor."

They did. We reached the fourth floor landing, and quietly, slowly opened the door leading to the hallway.

All seemed quiet. We stepped carefully into the hallway and closed the door. We were definitely in a research area. There was no one else around. Each doorway had a Project name over it. Names like "Project Dream Control," "Project Behavior Control," "Project Thought Control," and "Project Mind Control."

"What are they trying to do here?" I asked.

"They're supposed to be producing chemical products to help people. This looks like someone's planning a war to launch on the human race."

Just then an office door opened. Several men and women came out, and Lisa and I ducked into a doorway just before they saw us.

"We must solve the formula problem tonight!" one of the men said. "As long as that boy and girl are free, there is a danger we will be discovered and everything will be ruined."

"We must not let that happen," one of the women said. "We must not. The master will not stand for it!"

"Don't worry," another man said. "We will use those two children to find out why they are different. And when we've finished using them, we will destroy them!"

I peeked around the corner of the doorway. That last voice had sounded familiar. It was my father! Then he and the group used an ID card to enter the room marked "Project Mind Control" and closed the door behind them.

"Remember," Lisa said, practically reading my thoughts, "that wasn't really your father speaking. He's under control, like everyone else."

I stared at the door they had gone through.

"We have to go in there," I said, feeling my pulse quicken.

"Wait," Lisa said. "Before we do that, we might be able to learn something important in the room they just left."

Lisa had a good point. "Okay, let's take a look in there. And let's get out of this hallway before someone spots us."

We went to the door the group had exited. Lisa took her mother's ID card and slid it into the slot. There was a little screen next to the slot. A message on it flashed, "Enter Personal Code Number For Entry, Please."

"What's your mother's code number?" I asked Lisa.

"I don't know!" Lisa said. "I don't know anything about a code number! We're not going to be able to get in."

"Hold it," I said. "This is like one of those PIN numbers grownups use for banking. I know my parents use their birth dates for all their PIN numbers, so they won't forget them. What date was your mother born?"

"October 23rd," Lisa said.

"Tenth month, twenty-third day," I said. "Try punching in 1-0-2-3 on the machine."

Lisa hit the one, the zero, the two, and then the three. There was silence. And then there was the sound of a lock springing. The door was opening.

"Brilliant!" Lisa said, pushing the door open.

"I owed it to us, partner," I said. "If I'd had a better plan, they wouldn't have figured out where we were so quickly."

"Well, this makes up for it," Lisa said. We moved into the room. It was dark. I found a light switch on the wall, and flipped it on. Lisa let out a scream. I turned around. We were standing face to face with Jeffrey, the young pilot who had flown us to Keyserville!

10

Jeffrey's eyes were wide open, and they weren't blinking. He was standing straight up against the wall. I saw that a thin stream of blue-yellow gas was circling around his head. He was breathing in the gas.

"I know him," I said to Lisa. "He was our pilot." I stared at Jeffrey. He seemed to be unconscious, even with his eyes open.

"I wonder why he's here, and what they're

doing to him," Lisa said.

I stared at Jeffrey's eyes. And somewhere inside I felt a connection. Somehow I felt I heard Jeffrey calling to me to help him, and if I did, he could help us.

"I'm going to take a chance," I said.

"What?" Lisa said, alarmed. "Ricky, be careful."

I reached up and placed my left hand over the small vent the gas was coming from. I blocked the gas. In a matter of seconds Jeffrey's eyes fluttered. He coughed. Then he staggered away from the wall.

Lisa and I grabbed him as he fell forward.

"Lisa, you hold him while I block off this vent," I said. I grabbed a roll of tape that was on a nearby desk and ripped off several pieces and placed them over the vent. The gas could no longer get in.

Jeffrey was coughing and groggy, but he was waking up.

"Thanks, kids," he said. "I think you might have saved my life."

"Jeffrey, what's going on here?" I asked.

He stared at me. For a moment nothing happened. Then his eyebrows shot up. "Of course," he said, "you're the boy I flew in earlier today. It seems like it was days ago."

"When we landed you had some kind of a fit," I said. "You started screaming at us to get out of Keyserville, and before we knew it they were taking you away in a police van."

"They brought me here," Jeffrey said. "For further experiments."

"What kind of experiments?" Lisa asked.

"Do you kids have any idea what's going on in Keyserville? What's happening to the people here? Why it's an isolated community that can only be reached by plane? And what they're planning for the future?" Jeffrey asked.

"We know it has something to do with the gas that's being produced in this building," Lisa said, "that they're making everyone breathe."

"You got that right, young lady," Jeffrey said. "A gas that when it's breathed in causes people to give over control of their minds and wills."

"Who to?" I asked.

"To the gas," Jeffrey said. Lisa and I both stared at him, not sure we really heard what he had said.

"What you have here is an experiment that's gotten out of control. They were combining several new chemicals, hoping to produce a product that would help relieve human suffering, a gas which would eliminate all sorts of physical and mental ailments that afflict human beings."

"But it didn't turn out that way," I said.

"No," Jeffrey said, with a sharp laugh. "They accidentally created a gas monster, which when inhaled takes control of the human mind and turns it into a slave of the gas."

"A slave of the gas?" Lisa said. "You make it sound almost like the gas is a thing, that it's alive."

"It is," Jeffrey said, softly, staring at us. "It's alive, and it's getting stronger every moment."

"But how come we're not affected by it, Lisa and me?" I asked.

"And what about you?" Lisa added.

"We're the weak link in the gas's master plan," Jeffrey said. "You two much more than I am. I fall under its control and only from time to time am I able to regain my free will. I think it has to do with my deep-sea diving in my spare time. I inhale a lot of pure oxygen while underwater, and it's made my blood stream and lungs stronger than most people's. Pure oxygen seems to be one antidote to the gas."

He stared at me and Lisa. "But how does that

explain you two?" he asked. "The gas hasn't seemed to affect you at all."

"I don't know," I said, shrugging. "There's nothing very special about me."

"What do you mean?" Lisa said. "You have asthma, you use an inhalator."

"So?" I said, not wanting to make an issue of my asthma in front of Jeffrey. "You have diabetes, you take insulin every morning."

"I told you, it's no big deal," Lisa said.

"Wait!" Jeffrey said, standing. "It's a very big deal. The asthma spray, the insulin. They're acting like defense systems in your lungs and blood streams. That's why the gas hasn't affected you two! Does anyone else here know about this?"

"Mr. Lawrence knows I get insulin shots," Lisa said, "my mother, who's a research chemist here, told him."

"And Mr. Lawrence knows I use inhalators," I said. "He ordered my mother to destroy my supply earlier this evening. I'm down to just one."

"Kids, we have to get out of Keyserville and alert the authorities on the outside to what's happening here. And we have to do it tonight," Jeffrey stated.

"But I can't leave my parents," I said. "My father's in that room across the hall right now."

"And you know what he's doing?" Jeffrey asked. "He's working at the will of the gas monster. Working on finding a way to make the gas more powerful so even people who use inhalators or insulin or breathe in pure oxygen will no longer be immune to it. And when that happens, the gas will unleash itself on all of humankind, and the entire planet will become slaves to that yellow and blue gas."

"I'm not leaving this building without my father," I said.

"And how do you propose to do that, Ricky?" Lisa asked. "You heard what Jeffrey's told us. We have to get help from the outside, and then come back and rescue our parents and all the others."

"I'm not leaving without a fight," I said.

"And how are you going to fight?" Lisa asked.

"With this," I said. And I reached into my pocket and pulled out my inhalator.

11

"What are you saying, Ricky?" Lisa asked, as she and Jeffrey both stared in surprise at my very last plastic inhalator.

"If the spray works for me, it'll work for my dad," I said. "All I have to do is have him inhale some of the mist and it should release him from the gas's control."

"That's noble, Ricky," Jeffrey said, "but very dangerous."

"I won't leave without trying," I said.

"Okay, look, I understand how you feel, so let me make the following offer," Jeffrey said. "If you go straight out the back road leading away from the research center, you'll come to a swampy marshland. It's inside the Keyserville property, the only swamp land they haven't converted to suburbia yet. There's a one-engine plane there that I have the keys to. I'm going to leave this building and head for the plane now. I will wait exactly forty-five minutes. If you haven't shown up by then, I'm taking off without you. Do you understand?"

"Yes, Jeffrey," I said. "That's fair enough."

"Ricky, that's crazy, you'll never pull this off. Don't try it!" Lisa pleaded.

"I'm sorry, Lisa, it may be crazy, but that's my dad in that other room and you don't desert your parents when they need your help the most. You go with Jeffrey, and I'll try my best to be at the plane on time," I said in one long breath.

"No," Lisa sighed, "I'll stay and help you."

"Don't be crazy," I said.

"It may be crazy," Lisa replied, "but you don't desert your partner when he needs your help the most." She turned to Jeffrey. "Hold that plane."

"Forty-five minutes," Jeffrey said. "Good luck, kids."

Jeffrey shook each of us by the hand, then he opened the door and slid out into the hall.

"Well, we don't have any time to waste," Lisa said.

"Okay, partner," I said, "let's go for it."

We went out into the hall. We looked around. The long hallway was silent, empty. We carefully approached the door that led into the "Project Mind Control" area.

"Okay," I whispered. "The ID card."

Lisa slipped the card into the slot. The screen requested the user's code number. Lisa hit the four numbers of her mother's birthday. The screen read, "Incorrect Code. Please Re-enter."

"She has a different code for this entry!" Lisa said, with alarm.

"That makes sense," I said. "That way if

someone got her card, they'd have to know a series of access codes to get into the different secret areas." I smiled. "But I don't think she was ever counting on her own daughter being the one to use the card. So we have an advantage."

"What do you mean?" Lisa asked and frowned at me.

"When's *your* birthday?" I asked.

"My birthday? July eleventh. Why?"

"People will always use PIN numbers they can remember easily, right? So if this one isn't your mom's birthdate, there's a good chance she used her daughter's. July eleventh? That's the seventh month, eleventh day. Lisa, try zero-seven-one-one."

Lisa punched it in. The door slid open. We went in.

We found ourselves standing at the top-most row of a large arena. The seating area beneath us was empty. But down below, in the arena, was a sight that made me gasp.

"That's incredible," Lisa whispered.

We were staring down at a lit-up stage area. About twenty men and women sat in chairs in a circle around the stage. My father was one of them. I also noticed Mr. Lawrence. And the others all looked like chemists and researchers.

And in the center of the stage, what nearly took my breath away, was a huge glass-like dome structure. It was shaped like an enormous crystal ball. And filling the ball was a mass of blue-yellow gas. The gas was in constant motion within the glass dome. And it was speaking!

"When there was only the girl with the insulin protection, I was patient that a remedy could be found," the gas said. "But now with this new boy and his inhalator immunity, the situation for me becomes more urgent. An antidote must be developed! I demand it! For until we can be sure that every human being will fall under my control, I will not be able to begin my attack on all of humanity, to enslave the entire earth. Do you understand?"

"Yes, master!" they all responded as one voice.

"I'm going to move down there," I whispered to Lisa.

"I'm right behind you," she whispered back. As we carefully made our way down the rows of seats toward the stage below, the gas monster continued to give instructions.

"Doctor Daniels, what do your first calculations show?" the voice of the gas angrily demanded of my father.

"Of all humans, 98.73% are currently primed to become your slaves, master," Dad said.

Lisa and I were now about half-way down toward the stage area.

"That leaves a little over one percent who would still show resistance to your dominance, such as individuals inhaling asthma spray, using insulin, perhaps those on oxygen respirators, or anyone who regularly inhales pure oxygen. But I am confident with the minds and talent you have assembled here that we will very soon put an end to all resistance, and all of humankind shall lie at your feet, master!"

Everyone in the room applauded Dad's words. Lisa and I were just a few feet behind him. No one was aware of our presence. They continued to applaud Dad.

"Now!" I whispered loudly, both to Lisa and myself. I leaped onto the stage and shouted, "How about some applause for the resistance, folks!"

Everyone was stunned into silence. Dad opened his mouth in surprise. I aimed my inhalator directly down his throat. I pressed the top. Nothing happened. It was empty!

"Oh no!" I groaned.

"It's the boy and girl resisters!" Mr. Lawrence yelled.

"Don't let them get away, you idiots!" the gas roared. "Somebody grab them!"

"We've got to get out of here!" I shouted to Lisa, as everyone jumped up from their seats.

"I know," Lisa said, "but how? They're all coming after us. We'll never escape!"

"Maybe what we need here," I said, "is a small distraction." I grabbed a chair from the first row of seats, lifted it over my head, and flung it at the huge glass ball that held the gas monster, flung it as hard as I could. And waited. But not for long.

12

People were screaming and yelling. In moments the blue and yellow gas monster was released, filling up the room.

"Come on!" I said to Lisa, "this way!"

We ran back up the arena steps. I may have asthma, but as I'd proved with my twenty push-ups, I was in pretty good physical shape. And so was Lisa. The adults, when they realized what was happening, tried to run after us. But we were pulling away from them with each step.

"What about your father?" Lisa asked.

"Can't do anything about that now," I shouted. "We'll have to get to Jeffrey's plane and come back here with help. Help for all these people."

In moments Lisa and I were back out in the fourth floor hallway. We slammed the door behind us shut. And for good measure, I smashed in the code-entry device.

"Why'd you do that?" Lisa asked.

"They won't be able to open the door now and come after us," I said. "They'll have to use another exit. By then we'll be out of the building."

"Maybe the people won't be able to come through this door. But look at that," Lisa said, pointing. A thin steam of the blue-yellow gas was wafting up through a crack in the door.

"We can't worry about that, we've got a plane to catch," I said. I saw a clock on the hallway wall. We had only twenty-five minutes left before Jeffrey would take off. With or without us.

We quickly ran back down the stairway until we reached the bottom floor. There was a side door exit that led directly outside. I shoved the door open.

As Lisa and I stepped outside about ten uniformed and armed policemen came running at top speed toward us.

"Oh no!" I said.

"Take it easy," Lisa whispered. "Pretend you're mind-controlled."

The policemen pulled out their weapons and aimed them at us. In a remarkably calm, controlled voice, Lisa pointed back toward the building. "Officers, the boy and girl you're looking for are inside. They're up on the seventeenth floor."

"Thank you, young girl," an officer said, and they ran by us into the building.

"That was great," I said.

"A free mind will out-think a controlled mind every time," Lisa said. We began running down the road Jeffrey had told us to take.

Soon we found we were on a dirt road. This part of the community really hadn't been developed yet. There were no lights out here, but luckily there was a full Florida moon, which practically lit up the countryside, guiding us.

"How much time do you think we have left?" Lisa asked.

"Not very much," I said. "Just keep running." I gasped a little.

"Are you all right?" Lisa asked. Her voice was filled with alarm.

"I'm fine," I replied.

"You don't have any inhalator mist left," she said.

"Just keep running," I said. I didn't want to concern Lisa. The last thing we needed was my getting an asthma attack. A great deal of exertion like running could bring on an attack. But I couldn't worry about that now. We had to get to that plane.

Suddenly our feet were wet. "It's like a swamp out here," Lisa said.

"It *is* a swamp," I replied. "Keyserville is built on one big swamp."

"At least we can see pretty well," Lisa said. "I was afraid it was going to be pitch black out here."

"It's real bright," I said, as we continued to run and splash our way through the dank damp undergrowth.

Lisa glanced over her shoulder. "Ricky!" she shouted, nearly coming to a stop.

"What!" I said.

"Look! We've got company!"

I turned and looked back, and immediately

understood why the area was so well lit. It wasn't just the full moon. Running after us was a giant cloud of yellow-blue gas. It had re-formed itself, and was pursuing us!

"It can't hurt us. And it can't stop us. Come on," I said.

We kept running. My lungs were beginning to feel like they were on fire now. But I wouldn't give in to it. Nothing would keep me from getting on that plane.

"There he is!" Lisa cried.

Just beyond the next bog was the plane. Its lights were on, and Jeffrey had started the engine.

"Jeffrey, wait, it's me and Lisa!" I shouted out, my voice breaking.

"Hurry!" Jeffrey called back.

We dashed through the marsh and reached the plane, which was on the edge of the river area. Jeffrey opened the door and we scrambled in. Lisa hopped into the rear seat. I sat down in the front seat, next to Jeffrey.

"Buckle up, we're taking off right now!" Jeffrey said. As the plane moved over the river and began to climb, we quickly told Jeffrey what had happened.

Fright Time

He listened intently to our story. "Okay, we need to get military and medical personnel and supplies into Keyserville as soon as possible," Jeffrey said. "You have a community back there of people whose minds have been altered and they need attention and they need it fast. Meanwhile, what happened to the gas monster? I thought you said it had re-formed and was following you."

I glanced out the window as the plane began to fly over the dark Everglades below. The gas was nowhere in sight.

"Maybe it ran out of gas," Lisa said. This made both me and Jeffrey laugh.

Suddenly the gas rose and popped up from beneath us! It enveloped the entire plane. It had been hiding and waiting to attack us.

"It's trying to blind us!" Lisa said. "We'll crash!"

"No way," Jeffrey said. "I have terrific radar. We'll make it to Miami, gas or no gas."

"Then that's it!" I shouted. "We win!"

"We win!" Lisa responded, giving me a high-five from the back seat.

I turned to Jeffrey. "We win, right, Jeffrey?" Jeffrey didn't respond. He kept staring straight

64

ahead. "Jeffrey?" I asked, suddenly a little concerned. "Is everything all right?"

"Ricky!" Lisa shouted. "The gas has seeped into the plane! Look, it's entering Jeffrey's nose!"

I stared closely at Jeffrey. Lisa was right. Jeffrey was inhaling the gas. His eyes had turned that scary shade of yellow again.

Suddenly Jeffrey shouted, "Yes, master! Crash the plane! Those are your orders and I must obey!"

And we began to head nose-first toward the ground below!

13

"Ricky, do something!" Lisa screamed. "We're going to crash!"

What could I do? Jeffrey was far too strong for me to fight with, and he was gripping the wheel with all his might. We'd crash in about another fifteen seconds. This was a real emergency! Wait, I thought. Emergency. In a plane. Suddenly it all came back to me.

Oxygen!

FRIGHT TIME

I looked above me. There was the oxygen mask right over my head! I grabbed it, jammed it over Jeffrey's face, covering his mouth and nose, and pressed down hard on the "On" button.

I could feel the pure oxygen flowing into Jeffrey's body, down his throat, into his lungs.

Suddenly his body shook. His head veered violently. He pushed the mask away.

"I'm okay, I'm okay!" he said, and he pulled on the wheel. I looked down below. We were only about a hundred feet from crashing into the ground. We began to level off, and in moments Jeffrey had the plane heading back up again.

"That was fast thinking, Ricky," Jeffrey said. "We could have all been goners."

"Speaking of goners," Lisa said, looking out the window, "the gas is gone."

"And this time," I said, breathing easier, "I hope it's for good."

We landed in Miami shortly after that. Once we were on the ground, Jeffrey went to work, finding out just who in authority would listen to our story and do what had to be done to bring everything and especially everyone back to normal in Keyserville.

Don't Breathe

Lisa and I listened to him as he described the situation, giving each other quiet signs of relief. We both realized that without Jeffrey, we'd have been really sunk. I mean, who would have believed such a fantastic story coming from two kids? This way, there was a grown-up telling it all, and we were there to confirm it.

It was awesome to see the way everyone swung into action. State troopers, military, hospital emergency teams—it was like mobilization for a war. Only this time, it wasn't to defeat an enemy—it was to save a lot of good people. Like my mom and dad. And Lisa's.

They let us go back to Keyserville on one of the first helicopters. That way, we could show them where everything was. I never felt so strong or so important in my life. Here were all these guys, some of them in pretty impressive uniforms, asking us—Lisa and me, two kids, after all—not only where things were, but what *we* thought were the best ways to do what had to be done.

And best of all, they were decent enough to take us each to our own homes right away, and see that our parents got taken care of first. Then, after I knew everything was okay at my house, and I had explained it all to Mom and Dad, this really cool major let us come along to watch the rest of the town being put back in order.

All the residents were given pure oxygen to breathe, and everyone was restored to their former, normal selves. The gas monster was never seen or heard from again.

Mom, Dad and I decided to stay in Keyserville. The work that Dad had originally thought he was going to do at their chemical plant was still waiting to be done. Good work, developing chemical products that would benefit people, and this time making sure that none of the chemical experiments got out of control or did harm to anyone.

As for me, I'm having a great time at school. Lisa's my best friend, of course, but I've also made a lot of other new friends.

And about once a week Jeffrey takes me out for some underwater diving. It's really fun; the diving, the swimming, the underwater world. Come down and visit us sometime. The people are the friendliest. And the air is great.

OVERNIGHT-MARE

by Anne Wolfe

1

Matt took a quick look around. His friends Wayne and Jay stood by impatiently, burdened with camping gear, as he trained a flashlight on the sign hanging from the fence surrounding the New Market battlefield.

"Do Not Enter," Matt read. "I thought this battlefield was open to the public. I didn't know they closed it up at night."

Wayne moaned. "You mean to tell me we hiked all the way here from town for nothing?"

Matt carefully set one foot halfway up the woven wire fence to test it. "Not me, I'm going over." Though the wire sagged a little, the fence held his weight. He gripped the post with both hands, gingerly lifted himself up, and swung his right foot over the strand of barbed wire, hooking it into the other side. Awkwardly, he managed to vault into the deserted battlefield.

"Me next," Jay piped up, throwing Matt's gear over.

"It should hold you, but it might not hold Wayne," Matt commented. "Wayne, how much do you weigh?"

"None of your beeswax," Wayne grumbled. "It'll hold."

Thin, wiry Jay vaulted over, clearing the fence by two feet. Wayne grunted and groaned, scrambling over by degrees.

When all three boys cleared the fence, they set off at a run toward a cement culvert, which they had to pass through to get to the rocky field. A trickle of water ran down the curved pipe wall, but it was fairly dry. The interstate traffic noise overhead echoed all around them.

"You think we'll be arrested?" Jay asked, as if he might be looking forward to it. "Nobody I know ever camped out overnight on a real battlefield. It's against the rules."

"Nobody will see us," Matt answered. "There's not a soul around at this time of night."

They spent the next hour pitching a tent between two trees in an area lit by the beam of Matt's lantern. After unrolling their sleeping bags inside the tent, they huddled in their jackets, exhausted.

"Now we shall begin the evening's entertainment," Matt said, taking out a harmonica and waving it with a grand flourish.

"Ssssssh! I heard something." Wayne rolled slowly toward the open tent flap and peeked out into the darkness.

"Yeah, I heard Bigfoot," Jay scoffed, making monster claws. "He lurks in the deserted wilderness, and gobbles up trespassers like us for his dinner."

Matt inhaled, his harmonica poised near his mouth. "Cool it, you clowns. I want to play this song I made up. It's really cool."

"I swear, I heard something. Hey, pass the chips," Wayne interjected, lounging flat out inside the front flap of the canvas tent. "It's only eleven o'clock and we're almost out of food already. It's gonna be a long night."

Matt chuckled and accidentally wheezed into

the harmonica. "You probably heard Jay chewing with his mouth open."

Wayne sighed. "I know I heard something. This place gives me the willies. It's too quiet out here. How could you forget the boombox, Matt? It's gonna be boring as heck in here. We might as well just go to sleep."

Matt laughed. "I can't believe we're camping on the same place where over a hundred years ago, some battle happened right here in the Civil War."

"Hey, Wayne, I bet you heard a ghost out there. And I bet when they were camping out here back in the Civil War, they ran out of food all the time and didn't cry like babies," Jay added.

"I'm hungry," Wayne said with a sigh, "And this is *now*, not the last century. At least I wouldn't be bored if I was back there in the Civil War."

"No, because they'd use you for target practice," Jay teased.

Matt choked back a laugh and waved his harmonica. "I can't play my new masterpiece if you guys make me laugh. Cut it out."

Wayne sat up straight. "Now I *know* I heard something. Are there bears around here?"

"Yeah, teddy bears," Jay scoffed. "If you get too close, they hug you to death. So just close the flap."

Wayne peered out into the darkness again. "I can't see a thing."

"Use the flashlight." Matt passed it with his free hand.

"I won't be able to see anything with the lantern glaring in here. Turn it off a sec so I can shine the flashlight outside."

Jay punched the half-empty bag of chips.

"Sssssshhh. There it is again. Hear it?" Wayne held up a hand to signal silence. All three boys froze in place and listened.

A gunshot echoed in the distance, above the sound of the roaring traffic from the interstate.

"So? It's a gunshot," Matt scoffed. "Haven't you ever seen hunters around here?"

"No, they're not allowed," Wayne said.

"So, neither are we," Jay retorted.

Wayne stuck his head outside the open flap. "Who would be hunting at this time of night?"

"Vampires," Jay answered.

"Hey, don't laugh. I saw a show on TV where they interviewed real-life vampires," Wayne said, his voice barely audible inside the tent. "I bet there's even a cemetery around here."

"Yeah, but bodies could be buried anywhere," Matt said, thoughtfully. "If this was a battlefield, I bet there were hundreds, if not thousands, of dead bodies to bury. They couldn't carry every single corpse back home. Lots of them could've been buried right here beneath us, right where they died."

Matt inhaled deeply and surprised himself by producing a short blues riff on the harmonica.

"Yuck, dead bodies." Jay stopped chewing suddenly. "There goes my appetite."

Wayne pulled his head back into the tent and grabbed the bag of chips. "Good. Now there'll be more for me."

The boys sat a moment, each lost in thought, listening for more sounds from outside.

Two gunshots rang out closer to the tent.

"Somebody didn't like your music, Matt," Jay said.

Matt shivered uncontrollably in the night air. The shots seemed too close.

"Cool it, guys," Matt scolded. "Somebody's gonna hear us, and we're gonna get caught."

Wayne fell back, laughing and gasping. "Better we get caught than call a coyote convention with that har-de-harmonica of yours."

Matt leaned his elbows on his knees and closed his eyes, trying to forget the gunshot sounds. He played a few bars as Jay and Wayne looked on, their skeptical expressions changing to admiration.

"Not too bad," Wayne said softly. "Know any more tunes?"

Matt felt a warm flush of pride. He clenched his eyes shut again, and swayed with the rhythm of "Yankee Doodle."

Wayne and Jay sang out, "Yankee Doodle went to town, riding on a pony, stuck a feather in his cap and called it macaroni..."

Matt stopped suddenly and stared across the tent at his friends. He couldn't ignore the sounds any longer. Wayne and Jay abruptly shut their mouths.

"I heard it again," Matt whispered, extinguishing the lantern. "Turn off the flashlight."

Wayne grabbed it. Wrapped in total darkness, except for the distant rays of the interstate lights, the boys strained to hear.

"Sounds like we're in for a storm, is all," Matt whispered. "That must be what I heard."

"It's too dry for a storm," Jay insisted. "And

there isn't any rain or lightning."

"Matt's right. I heard thunder. That was definitely thunder. A major storm is coming our way, and here we are stuck in the middle of nowhere. We'll probably float away," Wayne said.

"Shush." Matt closed his eyes and strained to identify the strange sounds from the outdoors that now filled the tent. Still unable to pinpoint them, he felt bumps pop out on his arms and legs. To settle his jangled nerves, he slowly repeated the chorus of "Yankee Doodle."

Jay's wide eyes glistened from behind his thick glasses like two tiny pools. Wayne's heavy breathing rasped through the air.

"I just heard a voice," Matt said softly. "Did you?"

Jay nodded slowly. "I think so."

"Hey!" A voice shouted from outside. "Hey, you in there!"

Wayne gasped.

"Hey!" The voice was more insistent. "You in there!"

"Wayne, answer him," Jay said.

"No, you." Wayne clasped his knees to his chest as if he wanted to curl himself into a ball.

Matt crawled on his hands and knees to the

tent flap. Slowly, cautiously, he pulled it open and looked outside. "Give me the light."

Jay handed him the lantern. Matt switched it on low and held it up into the night. Its powerful beam revealed a shadowy figure leaning against a tree on the other side of a massive puddle near the tent, about five hundred yards away.

"Who—who's there?" Matt called timidly.

"Hey, you, boy!" A man's raspy voice shouted, "Why don't you play one of ours?"

"Excuse me?" Matt stammered.

"Play one of ours," the voice shouted impatiently. "You know 'Dixie', don't you? Play 'Dixie'!"

Matt glanced back at Wayne and Jay, who seemed frozen on the spot.

"Do what he says," Wayne grunted. "Play 'Dixie' for petesake."

"I don't know 'Dixie'," Matt whispered.

"You better learn," Jay grumbled. "This might be the creep Wayne was expecting."

Matt's eyes focused on the man. Like a photo slowly developing, more details emerged through the darkness. The man wore a ragged flannel shirt, ripped trousers, and boots. His left arm was bandaged and clutched against his chest in a primitive sling.

"He's just sitting there, and I think he's hurt," Matt whispered. "Come look."

Wayne groaned and rolled toward the opening. Jay stayed put.

As Matt held the flap open wide, Wayne wiggled up next to him and peered into the darkness.

"I don't see anything," Wayne said.

Matt looked at Wayne and pointed, "Right there, across the water, on the other side." He glanced over and rubbed his eyes. Then he blinked a few times to be sure.

No one was there now.

Before his very eyes, the man had vanished into thin air.

2

"I definitely saw someone," Matt insisted. "Right over there. I swear, he just—vaporized. He disappeared."

"Maybe he's a security guard," Wayne said, "and he went to go tell on us. I bet he's calling the police."

"Unless he is the police," Jay added.

"No way." Matt resumed his sitting position

and raised his harmonica. "Good thing he's gone. I don't think I can play 'Dixie'."

He experimented with a few tentative notes and soon picked out the tune.

Wayne zipped up the tent flap and burrowed his bulky body down into his sleeping bag. Jay rolled his eyes, then stared silently at Matt.

As his rendition of "Dixie" improved, Matt played it louder, wondering if he could tempt the strange man to reappear. Between choruses, he listened for the voice. He'd almost given up, when he heard it again.

"That's the poorest excuse for 'Dixie' I ever heard," the voice chided.

Wayne shot up, slithered out of his bag, and ripped open the flap, as if he intended to bolt.

The shadowy figure stood to one side of a tree across the water. One fist rested on his hip, and he appeared to be studying their tent.

Noticing the man's strange cap, Matt gasped.

"He's wearing a weird gray cap with a wide, flat bill," Wayne remarked, venturing into the opening.

Suddenly Jay called out, "A Confederate. He's wearing a Confederate cap!"

Matt mumbled, "Probably bought it at some

battlefield souvenir joint."

"Unless he's a ghost," Wayne joked.

Silence settled over the tent. The boys continued to watch the stranger watch them. Finally, the man shifted around and moved a few feet away to the other side of the tree, seeming to stumble over his feet.

Matt's eyes sharpened on the stranger. There was something holding him in place. A weight of some kind, tied to his ankle, was restricting his movement to the few feet around the front of the tree.

Suddenly he knew what it was. "A ball and chain," he cried.

"This is crazy," Jay said, shaking his head. "How did he get there in the first place? He wasn't there when we set up camp. He couldn't have walked here with a ball and chain."

"Really weird," Matt said, shaking his head. "Maybe we should try to talk to him."

"Not me," Wayne said, diving for his sleeping bag. "I'm not talking to anyone chained to a tree in the middle of nowhere."

Matt stared, transfixed, watching to see what the stranger did next.

The man appeared impatient. He leaned

against one side and then the other of the tree.

"What's wrong with that guy?" Jay said. "He acts like he's mad."

"You'd be mad, too, if you were chained out here in the middle of the night," Matt said.

From his sleeping bag, Wayne muttered, "Maybe he just doesn't like your choice of tunes."

The stranger's image began to flicker and fade.

"Whoa, do you see what I see?" Matt said, a quiver in his voice.

"He's disappearing," Jay said incredulously.

"Ohmigosh, he's gone. Is he there? Am I crazy or what?" Matt rubbed his eyes.

"He's not there," Jay said, removing his glasses to clean them. "He was there a minute ago, and now he's gone. Vanished. Kaput."

"Then Wayne was right. It is a ghost!"

"Yeah, and he's a Confederate, too. He had the gray cap. And those raggedy trousers."

"Okay, listen," Matt said. "He had an injured arm, wore raggedy old clothes and a Confederate cap, and had a ball and chain. Did you ever hear of any place today that uses a ball and chain?"

"Well, he could be an escaped prisoner —" Jay said.

"Yeah, I bet that's it." Matt leaped at the explanation. "It's got to be. But where did he learn to vanish into thin air like that?"

"He could be a magician, maybe," Jay offered. "They're always escaping and disappearing."

"But not on deserted battlefields in the middle of the night," Matt said. "It's got to be a ghost."

"Do you believe in ghosts?" Jay asked.

"No," Matt answered. "But now I'm not so sure. Ghosts usually haunt people because they want something, don't they?"

"How would I know?" Jay answered.

Matt stuck his head out into the darkness. "Hey, mister! Where are you? What do you want?"

Suddenly the voice replied. "I want something to eat, to see my mother and sister again, and I want to shed this blasted chain."

"Where is he?" Jay crawled up next to Matt.

"I don't know. Maybe he'll reappear." Matt cupped his hands around his mouth. "We can't see you!"

"Matt, play 'Dixie'," Jay whispered.

Matt played two whole choruses.

Slowly, a gray cloud of vapor rose from the edge of the water and snaked around the tree. The shimmering fog formed a vague human shape. Then details emerged, his face, clothes, the cap, and finally the ball and chain.

Jay punched Wayne and squealed. "You see this? I can't believe it!" He hollered out the tent, "Hey, you! Are you a prisoner?"

"That I am," the ghostly stranger answered with a hint of sarcasm. "Just a lowly deserter and bounty jumper unfit to wear the uniform."

Jay whispered, "He thinks he's a deserter and a prisoner. I bet he thinks he's still back in the Civil War!"

"He can't. The Civil War was over a hundred years ago," Matt added, shaking his head. "This is nuts."

"I'm going to sleep. I can't believe this," Wayne grumbled from his sleeping bag.

"What—What do you want?" Matt called out to the prisoner.

"Some rations, if you have any left, and a sharp sabre to cut these chains so I can get home to my mother and sister. They are all alone, and dangerously close to the Union army . . ." The stranger's pleas faded.

"Wayne, hand me the chips," Matt ordered.

Wayne didn't move. Jay grabbed the bag and tossed it to Matt. "You're gonna give him our chips?" he asked. "A ghost? You're giving our last crumbs of food to a ghost?"

"Why not, he's starving." Matt went out into the darkness, holding the lantern in front of him. "What's your name?" he hollered.

"Alexander Barton," came the reply, "son of the late Orlando Barton of Richmond. Who might you be? One of the Confederacy's fine musicians, I take it?"

"A musician? Oh, you mean because I was playing my harmonica? No way. I'm definitely not a musician, not officially, that is."

"A modest fellow, that's what you are," Alexander said, his tone becoming lighter. "How old are you, lad?"

"Twelve. Almost thirteen," Matt replied.

"Old enough to free me from the bondage of these chains?"

Matt didn't answer. He walked slowly and carefully around the water, afraid that Alexander might disappear at any moment.

"I have nothing to cut those chains with," Matt said. "But I brought you the rest of our food."

As he drew close to the ghostly man, Matt held the lantern between them. Alexander was translucent, allowing Matt to see vague shapes of the landscape right through him. His gray body shimmered and flickered as Matt stared, open-mouthed.

"You *are* a g—" he took a large gulp. "A g-ghost."

"Oh, am I so pale?" Alexander chuckled. "It's from hunger, then. You have some food?"

Matt held up the bag of chips. Alexander reached out with his good hand and took it, shaking it open and peering inside.

"What's that? Hardtack?"

"Huh?" Matt asked.

"Some newfangled biscuit? Not moldy, are they?" Alexander raised the bag and poured a few chips into his mouth. "I love biscuits, but the way my stomach is now, they could kill me. Lived on nothing but wild onions for days."

Matt watched, speechless, as Alexander gobbled down the rest of the bag. With an expression of ecstacy on his face, he gestured to the chain around his ankle.

"It's very rusty now, shouldn't take much work." He lifted his foot to show Matt.

Matt took out the army knife in his pocket, and bent over Alexander's foot to study the chain. "Seems like I could hack away at it right here," he said, "and it just might give way."

"That's the idea," Alexander said proudly. "I knew you could do the job. And whistle "Dixie" while you work, eh?" He had a weak but fairly hearty laugh.

Matt moved his hand over the ghostly chain, passing his fingers right through it. Then, as if playing a game of pretend, he moved his knife in a sawing motion. Though he felt sort of silly, he noticed that the chain was slowly giving way. Soon he made enough progress to finish the job by pretending to whack the chain with a heavy rock. Alexander was free.

"You can go now," Matt stammered. It occurred to him that maybe cutting the chain was what the ghost wanted, and that now he could stop haunting the battlefield and rest in peace.

Just then a rustling sound echoed across the water. Matt turned to see Jay coming around the puddle toward them.

When Alexander saw him, he disappeared.

"Jay!" Matt hissed. "What'd you have to do that for?"

"What?" Jay hissed back.

"Sneak up on him. He's gone now. And maybe he'll never come back. Oh well, I think I gave him what he wanted. I cut his chain."

"Rest in pieces, Alexander," Jay joked. "Now let's get back inside our sleeping bags and we won't talk or move till morning. I'm willing to bet Mr. Alexander Barton is just a big hunk of swamp gas."

"Swamp gas doesn't talk," Matt said, making his way back toward the edge of the water. "He mentioned something about hardtack, said it was like biscuits. He thought the chips were biscuits."

Suddenly, a shout echoed over the battlefield.

"There they are, boys!" A thunderous crash rocked the night. Shots of rifle fire popped above their heads. The sound of footsteps rushing toward them made them freeze.

"Run!" Matt yelled.

"Matt!" Jay shouted just as somebody threw Matt backward. Matt tumbled over the lantern, the wind knocked out of him. Jay fell on his side a foot away.

"Jay?" Matt whispered, reaching out and grabbing his hand.

"Yeah," Jay managed to say as his fingers clawed Matt's.

Together they stared up into the face looming over them. A Confederate soldier in full uniform, his face blackened by rifle powder, eyes burning like two red-hot coals, stood poised to hit them with his musket butt.

There wasn't even time to pray.

3

"They're growing Yanks small these days," the evil-looking soldier said, waving his hand in the air to signal to the others behind him.

"We're not Yanks," Matt stammered.

The lieutenant dropped his rifle to Matt's face. "If you're not Yanks, you'll still be taken for treason. You just turned Barton loose. He's a no-good deserter. Now our soldiers will be leaving in droves."

Three Confederate guards walked up and stared at Jay and Matt. "Have yourself a good look," the red-eyed soldier sneered. "See that they're fed and dispatch them to the prison. Turn them over there and get a receipt."

Each guard answered, "Aye, Lieutenant."

Matt looked at Jay and knew he was thinking the same thing. These were ghosts. How could they possibly be taken prisoner by a bunch of ghosts?

Matt decided to ignore them and return to the tent. He turned and began to walk toward the water, expecting Jay to follow close behind. When he didn't, Matt looked back to see Jay quivering in horror as the lieutenant held him by the arm.

"Hey!" Matt yelled. "You can't do that. We're not soldiers. It's 1995 and this is *not* the Civil War!"

The lieutenant let out a loud guffaw.

"Well then, if you're not soldiers, you're still traitors to the Confederate States of America, and you shall receive the punishment intended for Barton. Only if you find him and return him will you be able to save your scrawny necks."

The guards marched them further up the incline and tied them down against a tree. Then a guard threw pieces of cornbread at them.

Jay began to sniffle.

"Quiet there, Yank!" a guard barked. "I'm just dyin' to plug me a Yankee."

"Pick on somebody your own size," Matt grumbled.

His insolence was met with a tap in the back by a bayonet.

The guard sneered, "If we don't plug you, you'll rot away slowly, inside out, in prison." He walked away, laughing.

Matt prayed that the guard would disappear, that all the ghosts would quickly vanish.

No such luck.

The guards moved to lounge on a fallen log about 200 yards away, their rifles perched on their knees.

"They're gonna shoot us, Matt. I don't believe it, a bunch of ghosts are gonna shoot us!" Jay wailed.

"Maybe Wayne can save us," Matt said. "He's right over there. He must be able to see all this from the tent."

"We're too far away. He can't hear us yell, and besides, he's probably sleeping by now."

"We must do something, like get that deserter back, so we can go free." Matt strained against the ropes on his hands.

"If he was any kind of good guy, he'd free us the way we freed him," Jay grumbled.

"We should've made a run for it when we had the chance," Matt said.

"Not with our hands tied behind our backs and fastened to these tree trunks. No way," Jay sighed.

Moving his hands up and down, Matt attempted to saw the ropes against the rough tree bark. When he felt the ropes begin to fray a bit, he sawed harder and faster. He saw that one of the guards was watching him closely.

Suddenly Jay screamed. "Owwwww! My head itches." He rubbed his head against the tree. "I think there are bugs in my hair. My scalp is burning."

The guard forgot Matt for the moment and focused on Jay. Matt sawed as hard and fast against the tree as he could.

The guards laughed at Jay's discomfort and pointed, slapping their knees, nearly setting off a rifle accidentally.

"Watch where you aim that thing," Jay hollered. "You've got to untie my hands. I have to scratch my head. It hurts!"

Matt silently thanked Jay for distracting the guards with his yelling. He leaned forward and grunted, concentrating on freeing his hands.

Jay kept up his charade. "Help! Help! I'm going insane. It itches and burns so bad! Help me!"

Matt felt one of the ropes break. He sawed until another broke, and another. Then he leaned back against the tree and carefully untangled his wrists from the ropes, keeping an eye on the guards.

When both of his hands were finally free, he wasn't sure what to do next. For a moment, he sat thinking. Whatever he did, those guards would shoot him in a heartbeat.

But they were ghosts. Could he really be killed by ghosts' rifle fire? Should he give it a try and see? No. If his hands were tied by ghostly ropes, his body could be stopped by a ghostly bullet.

He had to help Jay now. Jay was bluffing to keep the guards distracted, but they were catching on to his ploy. Their trigger fingers might get itchy.

"Alexander Barton, where are you?" Matt whispered, calling to the deserter who had gotten them into this mess. He was probably in the next county by now, most likely haunting the house where his mother and sister lived a century ago. If not, he may have managed to "pass on" peacefully now that he had his freedom.

Suddenly Matt remembered that Barton had asked him to play Dixie. With an eye on the guards, he whistled softly, one chorus, then two. Within seconds, the guards fixed their eyes on something beyond the nearby trees.

Alternately squinting and jabbing each other, they pointed at something or someone.

A grayish white cloud drifted into sight between the trees. It covered the ground and reached toward the guards with long, twisting fingers.

"I bet Barton's back," Matt said in a stage whisper meant for Jay to hear.

Then they saw him. The cloud spiraled upward and the ghost stepped forward into the clearing in front of the guards, waving a white handkerchief. The men jumped up, pinned his arms in front of him, and pushed him on the ground.

While the guards wrestled with Barton, Matt crawled over to Jay and untied his hands.

Before long, Barton was bound and gagged.

Jay and Matt looked on, wondering if the guards were busy enough with their other prisoner to try to make a run for it.

"Let's go," Jay hissed. "Now."

Matt hesitated. "We can't leave him here like that."

"Are you crazy?" Jay shouted. "I'm leaving." He stood up and ran toward the water.

Matt lingered a moment and watched Barton

struggle. Barton's eyes widened at the sight of him, and he jerked his head sideways as if to signal that Matt should get away and go with Jay.

Instead, Matt picked up the ropes that had tied his hands and walked stealthily toward the guards, whose backs were turned to him as they taunted Barton.

Draping one rope over his shoulder, Matt held the other up to shoulder height, pulling it tight between his hands, and sneaked up behind the closest guard.

Barton's eyes betrayed his terror as he shook his head at Matt.

Matt felt someone grab the extra rope off his shoulder. Wheeling around, he saw Jay holding it just as he did. Without a word, they sneaked up behind the guards and whipped the ropes around their bodies, tieing their arms to their sides.

As the guards shouted, gasped, and stamped their feet, Barton continued to shake his head to say "no."

Jay and Matt exchanged worried glances, as their struggle to control the guards became more difficult.

"What do we do now?" Jay hissed. "I'm not about to commit murder, even if he is a ghost."

"How can it be murder if he's already dead?" Matt replied.

"I don't want to do this!" Jay's voice broke. "I don't want to be here. I want to go home!"

"Maybe this is just a dream," Matt said, hoping to calm him down. "If it is, don't worry, it'll be over soon."

"I'm letting him go," Jay cried. "I can't do this any more."

"If only Barton could move, he'd help us." Matt glanced at Barton's uncomfortable gyrations as he struggled to free himself. For a moment, Matt weakened his hold on the guard. In two seconds, the guard had his hands free. Turning quickly, his fist poised to punch Matt, the guard dropped suddenly to the ground and vanished into a dusty haze.

Matt stared open-mouthed at Jay, who also loosened the cord around the guard he'd been holding. In seconds that guard, too, vanished. "What happened?"

Without an answer, Jay turned and ran toward the water.

Matt untied Barton. Three seconds later, Barton flickered, turned stark white, and disappeared. "Wait!" Matt cried.

Lying flat on the ground to catch his breath, Matt gazed up at the moon, totally confused. Suddenly, it was night again, pitch dark instead of foggy moonlit gray. His lantern was somewhere near the water. On his hands and knees, he crept over the field in the darkness and found the place where he'd fallen over it earlier. It had rolled into the shallow water, but it lit the area enough to show Jay, doubled over at the water's edge.

"You okay?" Matt asked.

Jay sputtered and choked. "I was sick."

"You ate too many chips, that's all," Matt said, glancing around in the foggy darkness. A damp gray haze hung over them and moved slowly through the trees, slithering, twisting, and spiraling all around. Matt stood, paralyzed, watching for mysterious vapor clouds that might become ghosts.

"We almost died, Matt," Jay said, crying. "I can't believe we almost died."

"We're okay," Matt whispered. "We saved Barton and he saved us. We're even. It's over." He said it, but he wasn't really sure.

Somehow he suspected it was far from over.

He just wasn't sure *how* far.

4

The boys huddled uncertainly, standing in the dim light of the lantern, glancing around nervously, too terrified to move. They knew that something was about to happen, but they didn't know what.

Gunfire roared suddenly over their heads. The sound of men swearing and snapping whips made Matt and Jay whirl around to face a smoky haze that oozed from the woods. When the smoke lifted a bit, the dense foliage beyond had totally disappeared, replaced by a large open field of moving creatures making strange sounds. The scene sharpened slowly before their eyes.

A heavy cannon rolled onto the field, pulled by two ghostly mules. Scattered beside it and behind, rows and rows of Confederate soldiers and young cadets stood, with guns, rehearsing drills in small groups, often pointing their guns across the water toward the boys' tent.

When Matt glanced back at the tent, it vanished completely. He rubbed his eyes. Where their tent was supposed to be, he saw four primitive wedge-shaped army tents situated around a long wooden table, where a group of disheveled, rowdy men smoked, ate, and played cards.

"What's happening? Where are Wayne and the tent?" he cried.

Jay couldn't answer.

There was a volley of gunfire from behind the tents, amidst the sound of voices shouting and men running.

"You think Wayne's okay?" Jay stammered.

Matt let out a shaky sigh. "This has to be a bad dream. It has to. We'll close our eyes once more and when we open them, our tent will be there."

"It's no use." Jay's voice rose. "Our tent disappeared and so did Wayne. Now we'll never get back. We're trapped in the middle of the war!"

"We have to run for cover!" Matt shouted. "They're firing all around us. We could get hit!" He grabbed Jay by the arm and led him to some nearby trees. As they dropped panting to the ground beneath a bush, Matt felt something nudge him in the ribs.

He looked up into the bright red eyes of the same nasty lieutenant who had captured them earlier.

The man's body reeked with the smell of

sweat and smoke. "We're going into the line of battle, boys," he sneered. "I'm offerin' a grand opportunity for you to make amends and save your little skins. Atten-hup!"

Matt and Jay stood up slowly. Jay managed an awkward salute when Matt poked him in the ribs with his elbow.

The lieutenant pointed to a place beyond the dense woods and underbrush just ahead. "About half a mile up that way is a wall of felled trees, with heavy foliage facing us. I've got to march my men past those trees this instant, there's no time awastin'." He stood tall and leaned over the boys. "But it's too quiet up there. I don't like it."

Matt exchanged puzzled looks with Jay.

The lieutenant continued. "I figure you owe me a favor, because I didn't send you off to the pokey earlier for going soft over Barton. I'm letting you go free. You're free, right?"

Matt nodded slowly, though he felt anything but free at the moment.

The lieutenant stood back. "Now, I have to get my men and these cadets through those upturned trees. The only way I can do that is to march 'em in columns of four, which would mean a massacre if there's a Union trap waiting for us.

And I think there might be. There isn't a flag in sight, and I don't hear rifles. Something's fishy. I think the enemy is holed up back there waiting to get us."

Matt felt a light bulb come on in his brain. He knew what the lieutentant was telling them to do. Foil an ambush. The lieutenant wanted the two of them to be guinea pigs, live bait for a possible trap, to help him save his men and the younger soldiers, the ones he called "cadets."

"Now it could very well be a deserted enemy fortification of some sort." The lieutenant put on a crooked, toothless smile, which made him look so scary Matt heard Jay gasp. "In which case, there will be no enemy and we can pass on by without incident. But why should I risk 200 men and those fine young fightin' boys when you two can act as scouts and sneak in and out of the area? You report back to me personally as to your findings."

Soon, a commanding figure approached the lieutenant on horseback. "What's wrong, Lieutenant Miles? Why are you stopping? You're holding up the entire division."

The nasty, red-eyed Lieutenant Miles pointed out the narrow passage and its obstruction of trees. "I'm afraid, colonel, that it's a trap. If I send my men and boys through there, they may all be easy targets for the waiting enemy. I just can't do it." He whispered something to the colonel.

The colonel turned his horse toward Matt and Jeff. He gestured toward the four lines of soldiers forming behind him. "Well, boys, we cannot stay here. You fine cadets must help us move ahead. It is a tribute to your academy that you have volunteered to go through the timber and find out what is beyond it. Are you ready?"

Matt looked at Jay and mouthed "cadets?" Jay answered with a shrug and a shake of his head.

The colonel continued. "You are to advance through the woods about fifty feet apart. Make your way silently through the underbrush and fallen timber without being observed. Determine the position of the enemy and report to Lieutenant Miles, who will be waiting."

Matt stood dazed, at attention, and nodded numbly. Jay saluted the colonel and knocked off his glasses in the process. He scrambled to pick them up.

The colonel smiled for a moment, then resumed his solemn expression. "Carry your rifles and be ready to fire the minute you see an enemy soldier."

"Excuse me, sir," Matt interrupted. "We have no rifles. We don't know how to shoot."

The lieutenant and colonel both stared, looking horrified.

"The academy hasn't given you proper instruction?" the colonel asked incredulously.

The boys looked at each other. "What academy might you be referring to?" Matt asked.

The colonel frowned. "I thought all you boys were from Virginia Military Institute. You mean you're not from those cadets drafted to help the South win the war?"

Matt struggled with the possibility that, if they weren't cadets, they might be considered traitors again. To Jay, he whispered, "It's better to be cadets than traitors, right?"

Jay nodded.

Before Matt could explain, the colonel waved a hand impatiently. "Take two rifles. You'll learn as you go. Don't shoot yourselves or each other. If you see an entire enemy army, one of you must climb a tree and wave his cap as a signal to advance our troops."

"We don't have caps," Matt said.

The colonel reached into his saddlebag as his horse pranced in a circle, and produced two wornout gray, wide-billed caps and slapped them on their heads.

Moving forward together, Matt and Jay entered the woods some two hundred yards away. Creeping apart slowly, they separated to what seemed like the required fifty yards, till they could barely see each other. They heard only the sound of the bushes rustling as they advanced on the fort of fallen trees.

Suddenly, something leaped out from behind a bush and grabbed Matt, pulling him to a standing position. A Union soldier in full blue uniform held a rifle on him and ordered, "Surrender, lad."

Matt's mind raced with indecision. Should he surrender and let the colonel's Confederate army be killed? Would he be taken to some horrible prison by the Union army? What would happen to Jay? No matter what he did, it seemed that they'd both be killed by an army of ghosts! Doomed forever to remain with them in the Civil War, on this very battlefield! To haunt the place as ghosts themselves!

Without a second thought, Matt raised his rifle toward the sky, fired, then turned and ran. At least fifty gunshots echoed back at him from close range. He paused a moment to see if any found their mark. He was unharmed. Suddenly, Jay appeared at his side.

"Get down!" he ordered Jay. Taking off at a run, Matt dodged rifle fire and climbed the first tree he saw with almost unbelievable speed. Once safely anchored high up in its branches, he gazed back toward the Confederate camp and spotted the colonel's shiny black horse. Frantically, he waved his cap in the agreed signal, and fervently hoped Jay had managed to run for cover.

After the colonel acknowledged his signal, Matt climbed down from the tree and ran back toward the waiting Confederate troops. Forcing himself forward, out of breath, with a pain in his side, he soon found Jay. Without a word, he put a hand on Jay's shoulder. Together they pushed through the woods and fell gasping in front of the mounted colonel. Matt clutched his side and the pain soon went away, leaving him glad it was from overexertion and not from musket fire.

"Well done, mighty cadets." The colonel smiled for a brief second, then fixed a solemn frown on his face and turned his horse toward his troops. For a moment, the horse stopped short, and his forelegs moved ahead while his hind legs tried to retreat.

Matt knew just how the poor horse felt as the colonel wrestled him forward.

Responding to the colonel's hand signals, the four columns of men hoisted their rifles and marched quietly into the woods toward the fort.

"They're going to be killed," Jay whispered. "We all are."

Matt worried about the colonel, and hoped nothing horrible would happen to him. He put his arm around Jay's shoulder. "No, we won't be killed. Not us. We're not going to follow them. When the soldiers start moving out of the area, we'll sneak off and hide till they disappear."

If only they *would* disappear. Into thin air. This nightmare had to end soon!

"I'd feel better if I could see our tent," Jay said, his voice quivering. "I'd give anything to see stupid Wayne again. I wonder if *he* can see *us*, wherever he is. I'd even be happy to listen to him complain."

"Don't worry, think positive." Matt sighed. "Did you ever hear of anybody disappearing on one of these battlefields? This isn't like the Bermuda Triangle, though these ghosts definitely seem to vanish into thin air. If we're stuck here with a bunch of ghosts, they have to disappear eventually, at dawn or something, right? Then we'll be fine. We can go home. We'll wake up. Whatever."

Jay shivered. "Maybe people *do* disappear here. Kids are missing all over the country. Maybe those missing kids get swallowed up by armies of ghosts to fight in some old battle. Maybe we'll never get home again."

"Whatever you do, don't cry." Matt knew if Jay started to cry, he'd be joining him. The last thing he wanted to be was a helpless crybaby.

An explosion rocked the earth beneath their feet. Rifle fire blasted overhead. All around them, thunderous booms and explosions roared in their ears as the Confederate army moved forward past the fallen trees to meet the Union army head on. Fireworks lit the sky above. The sounds of men shouting and groaning made the boys cling to each other and crouch down in the semi-darkness.

From up ahead, a bugler sounded the "charge," and the boys watched from behind a tree as musket balls swept the field, throwing up little puffs of dust where they hit the dry earth in front of them.

OVERNIGHT-MARE

Suddenly, Barton appeared beside them, toting a rifle. Pulling two white handkerchiefs out from beneath his sling, he said hoarsely, "Tie these on your left arms, boys." He shook his head sternly. "You musicians have to wear these or get yourselves shot. No need to be heroes. These will keep you out of the war. Put them on and stay alive."

Matt grabbed a handkerchief, puzzled that Barton thought they were musicians, and the colonel had called them cadets. Why couldn't anyone see they were just a couple of ordinary kids? He tied the white cloth onto his sleeve and helped Jay do the same.

"Thanks," Jay said wearily.

"Do you think this will all be over soon?" Matt asked Barton.

Barton sighed. "One way or the other. It's already over for some."

Beneath the roaring gunfire and blazing sky, Barton crouched against a tree, lowered his head, and moved his lips as if in prayer. Then he rose, hoisted his rifle, and looked at the boys closely for a minute.

"Why aren't you on your way back to your family in Richmond?" Matt asked.

Barton frowned and looked up at the sky with misty eyes. "They're all gone."

Matt and Jay crawled over to him. Matt tried to think of some comforting words to say. There weren't any. He realized that Barton was rejoining the army and going into battle because he had no one else to worry about and nothing to lose.

Four more cannons rumbled past them. A pair of Confederate soldiers carried a wounded comrade over their crossed rifles. The air smelled of sulfur.

Barton muttered, "May God have mercy on our guilty souls," and jogged away.

A huge black horse rushed toward them in a panic, its nostrils flaring, eyes white with fright.

Jay pointed. "It's the colonel's horse. Without the colonel!"

Matt's mind went suddenly blank, as if a candle had blown out.

Lieutenant Miles approached and shouted at Matt, "Private, the colonel is in trouble! Rescue him if possible!"

OVERNIGHT-MARE

*Private! The lieutenant called him "Private,"
as if he was a real soldier!* Leaning his rifle
against a tree, Matt turned back toward the
Union ambush without another thought. In a
stooping run, he moved from bush to bush and
hid behind trees until he spotted the colonel on
the ground, pulling himself toward the shelter of
a low-hanging bush.

"Colonel!" Matt hissed. "The lieutenant sent
me to rescue you."

The colonel seemed disoriented and looked all
around, blinking in the smoky air. Suddenly, he
fainted, his eyes rolled back, and he fell onto the
ground.

Matt leaped to his side and whispered, "Stay
awake! Colonel, get up!"

Seizing the half-conscious officer by the
wrists, he began to drag him across the field,
sometimes tripping over other soldiers who had
fallen. He tried not to look at them, because if he
did, he might stop and cry, and he wouldn't be
able to save anybody, including himself. Because
of the thick, low-hanging smoke, Matt couldn't
tell if they were Union or Confederate soldiers.
The noise of the discharging muskets was deaf-
ening, and he couldn't recognize anyone except

the colonel.

"Bates," the colonel murmured. "Call me Bates."

"Mr.—er, Colonel Bates," Matt stammered, "can you walk?"

The colonel opened his eyes a second and shook his head, pointing to gaping wounds in both his legs.

Colonel Bates was surprisingly heavy, considering he was a ghost. Matt had to stop every few seconds to rest. Slowly and steadily, he managed to haul the colonel across the field and back about half a mile behind the battle lines. Before he was even aware of the distance he'd covered, Matt spotted a small group huddled around a waiting stretcher.

Jay paced nervously nearby, chewing his fingers, looking both frightened and angry, and sniffling back tears.

Nasty Lieutenant Miles appeared and barked, "About time. Glad to see you learned to obey orders," and stomped off.

The stretcher-bearers whisked Colonel Bates off toward the medical tent at the edge of their camp.

When the boys were finally left alone, Jay fell

against Matt and wailed hysterically, "What's the matter with you? You left me out here in the middle of the war all alone so you could rescue some ghost! Are you crazy? Look at me!" Jay shouted. "I'm alive. Look! Touch my arm! Flesh and blood!"

Matt stood, dazed and paralyzed, waiting for Jay's tantrum to run its course.

"You go out there and risk your butt and mine, to save some ghost *who's already dead*! You got that? Everyone out here but you and me is *already dead*! As doornails!" Then he slumped to the ground.

Matt felt a nervous laugh work its way up from deep down inside. He tried to swallow it, but it kept rising, up, up, up, till it reached his face and his voice, till he started laughing and couldn't stop.

"You think this is funny?" Jay screamed. "I'll show you just how funny I think it is!"

He pulled back his fist and shot a punch that missed its mark. Instead of hitting Matt's chest, Jay's fist soared into thin air and pulled him flat on his face, his glasses flying.

Matt reached down and helped him up, then retrieved his glasses. His laughing fit subsided. Trying to find the right words, he looked Jay in the eyes and said, "He's not dead. I think I just saved the colonel's life."

Jay's eyes widened in horror and he took a step back. "You—you *are* crazy! You've gone totally nuts. You think you're some kind of a soldier now, don't you?"

Matt shrugged. Maybe Jay was right. Maybe he was nuts.

"You do!" Jay screamed. "You're so puffed up and full of yourself now, you really think you're some kind of hero! I bet you even expect a medal! Well, look here! I'll give you a medal."

He glanced around and picked up the lid from an old rations tin and held it up in front of Matt.

Matt squinted at the label on the lid. "It says sardines."

Jay threw it down. "It should say weenies, because that's what you are. A weenie!"

The trace of a smile crossed Matt's face. "You're making me hungry."

Jay relaxed suddenly, letting his body go limp. "I give up. I don't know what to do, I don't."

Matt frowned. "There's a battle raging only a mile away from here, and we're on the wrong side. The South lost the war, you know. That means there's a good chance we'll be wiped out along with these ghosts."

"Is it my imagination, or is it getting darker?" Jay asked, looking at the charcoal gray sky.

"It's the middle of the night, isn't it?" Matt glanced around, confused. At times, it seemed like a cloudy overcast day, and at other moments, it seemed to be night. When the sky was at its darkest, the ghostly army appeared more transparent, and faded to dull gray colors.

Suddenly a sense of panic overtook the camp. One of the men hollered, "Enemy approaching from behind! Grab the horses! Fold the tents! Don't forget your guns!"

The sky blackened and rain began to fall, slowly at first, then in sharp torrents that lashed at the boys' faces and soaked their clothes. In minutes, the camp was awash in a sea of muck. Soldiers on horses stumbled about, tearing apart their resting places, throwing bedrolls, blankets, scraps of food, and firewood in their wake. Many soldiers slipped and fell, rising from the ground completely covered in mud.

Shivering from the cold rain, Matt said, "They're attacking up ahead and they say they're being attacked from behind, but they're not moving out. They're falling all over each other like clowns in a circus."

"What do you mean 'they'? It's us too! We're all going to be attacked!" Jay snapped.

Some of the men stared out in the direction where the enemy was supposed to approach. The veiled moonlight gave the battlefield an eerie glow, lighting up the cannons and horses that now stood deathly still beneath the trees.

A muffled sound caught Matt's ear. He put his hand on Jay's arm. "Ssssh. Listen."

Thunderous hoofbeats echoed in the night, rising in volume as they drew closer. A shadowy figure appeared suddenly in the forest path. It seemed to be made of smoke, and had no definite shape or outline.

"The headless horseman!" Jay gasped.

Matt shushed him. "No, it's not. Just watch and listen."

The shape of a man on horseback emerged, with others right behind him. His rifle glowed in the dark.

Matt threw down his cap and hissed, "Let's get out of here!"

Jay stood dazed with fright. Matt grabbed him and pulled him out of plain sight and into the trees.

"Come on, climb!" Matt leaped up into the tree and held out an arm to Jay. With a half-hearted jump, Jay tried to get a toehold in the lowest branch and missed. He pulled Matt back down onto the ground with him.

"Ouch! Can't you climb a tree?" Matt groaned. "Here, I'll give you a leg up. You go first." Making a basket with his hands, he boosted Jay into the tree and then followed him into the shelter of the branches.

Suddenly, someone yelled "Fire!"

Matt counted almost a hundred flashes and heard as many gunshots. He saw the shadowy man fall down out of the saddle. Someone shouted, "Good! We've got him! Wait for the rest!"

But the rest never came.

The soldiers waited, guns poised to fire.

The boys waited, shivering, high up in the tree.

Nobody said a word for a long time. There was no sound, not the whisper of a leaf, only perfect stillness.

Before long, the soldiers began to creep stealthily around the camp and approach the fallen man. When they got to him, the moon revealed him clearly. He was lying on his back, with his arms spread out at his sides. His mouth was open and his chest was heaving with long gasps. His white shirt was splashed with mud.

"They're gonna finish him off," Jay whined. "They're gonna shoot him right there on the ground."

"Shush." Matt felt his knees knock together and his teeth chattered.

The first soldier to reach the man stood still a moment. Then, putting down his rifle, he bent down to stroke the man's forehead. Then the others joined him in comforting the fallen man. They fussed over him and tried to help him, saying things like "I'm sorry," and "This wretched war."

Matt thought that they had forgotten the man was their enemy. He might leap up at any moment and kill one of them.

The wounded man muttered something about his wife and child. The others around him spoke soft comforting words to him, reassuring him that he would live to see his family again.

"I bet he's a spy," Jay whispered. "He's going to attack them when they're not looking. Just when they think he's harmless, he'll let 'em have it."

"Why isn't he in uniform?" Matt asked. "He's got a Union hat tucked in his belt, but that's all."

"He's like an ordinary guy to them," Jay answered. "He's just like one of them. Maybe that's why they can't kill him."

"Maybe that's why they can't kill us," Matt said softly, untying the handkerchief around his arm and using it to blow his nose.

The pelting rain fell harder through the trees, soaking through their clothes to the skin.

"If the ghosts don't kill us, we'll die of pneumonia out here," Jay complained.

Deep in thought, Matt said, "For a while I completely forgot that all those people down there are already dead."

Jay held out his hand. "I've been trying to tell you that, dude. It's nice to have you back in the real world."

Matt shook Jay's hand. "Yeah. So, you think they're winning?"

Jay rolled his eyes. "Not a chance. Like you said, we already know, the North won the war."

Rain washed into the camp and flooded the grounds, and everyone ran for cover.

Settling into the upper branches of the tree, Matt said, "We're better off up here beneath these branches than anywhere else."

Jay nodded numbly, his glasses completely steamed and dripping. "I can't see a thing."

Just then a giant crack of thunder shook the trees. Matt hugged the trunk and yelled, "Hold on tight!"

A long thin finger of lightning reached down from the sky and zapped the middle of the battlefield, sending blue sparks in every direction. Amidst shouts and neighing horses, the lightning struck again a few hundred yards away.

Jay shivered. "What are we doing in this tree? If it gets hit, it will split in half."

"Don't even think that. Just hang on," Matt ordered, shouting over another thunderbolt. "This storm can't last forever."

"Neither can this battle," Jay muttered. "When will it be over?"

"Sooner than we think! Look over there, across the water!"

Jay squinted through his foggy glasses. "What?"

"Our tent! I can see our tent again! The pup tents disappeared in the last blaze of lightning!

Holy cow! I can't believe it!"

Jay laughed, then let out a loud whoop. "Let's go! Now, before we get killed! Come on!"

"Not yet," Matt said. "Let's wait for the storm to pass. Let's just look around and watch what happens. It may be our last chance to see the war."

"No way! Please let it be over!" Jay cried.

The ghostly figures below began to flicker and fade with the departing lightning, from gray to white to black. Hundreds of shadows peppered the battlefield like a colony of ants, working, running, moving away, slowly, quietly, their shouts dying with the passing storm.

"Matt, guess what!" Jay exclaimed. "It stopped raining! And the thunder is far, far away now. Hear it?"

Matt nodded and looked around sadly at the field that was now a fast-moving haze. In a moment of inspiration, he whipped his harmonica out of his pocket. Lifting it to his mouth, he blew. Streams of water gushed out with no sound.

"Don't you dare play "Dixie"! If you do I'll punch your lights out!" Jay shrieked.

Matt shook out the water and dried the harmonica on his jacket. When he blew into it again, not a single sound came out. "Darn!" he muttered. "You'd think these things would be waterproof."

"What do you expect from cereal boxtops?" Jay chided. "Give it up."

Matt glanced around the grounds below, hoping to see Alexander Barton or Colonel Bates. The battlefield was totally empty now, with no traces of the horrors they'd endured. A low-lying fog hung all around and extended its snake-like fingers toward them. Their tent stood wet and silent across the massive puddle that had now swollen to the size of a small lake.

"How are we gonna get over there?" Jay asked. "The water's about a mile wide now."

"We can walk around it or swim over it. What do you think?" Matt grunted and began a slow descent from the top of the tree.

"If I were a ghost, I could float over it," Jay said wistfully.

"I'm gonna swim. What the heck, I'm already soaked," Matt said bravely.

"Okay. It's your call," Jay said, following Matt down the tree.

Slowly, wearily, the boys trudged to the edge of the water. A hint of morning sun peeked from behind the dark gray clouds, then disappeared, leaving the field in misty darkness again.

Stripping off his sneakers, Matt put a foot into the murky water. "Yikes, it's freezing. There's only one way to do this." He rolled up the legs of his jeans, zipped up his jacket, and prepared to dive.

"One Mississippi, Two Mississippi, Three Mississippi..." he counted, then took a huge gulp of air. "Here goes!"

The loud splat of his bellyflop echoed into the trees. Raising his head out of the muddy water, Matt yelled for Jay to jump in.

Jay laughed and went in after him, executing a clean head-first dive.

Feeling like a whale jumping out of the sea, Matt popped up and gulped in as much air as he could. He heard the distinct sound of shots being fired.

The battle wasn't over!

Jay snorted, gasped in a mouthful of air, and said, "Next time the sign says Do Not Enter, I'm not gonna enter. I'm gonna obey the rules, because that's what got us in trouble. We shouldn't have been out here on this battlefield in the first place. None of this would've happened..."

"Don't forget, this was all your idea. Stupid Wayne was the only smart one in the group," Matt muttered.

"Sometimes being lazy pays off," Jay said. "Wayne's probably snoring away right now."

At the edge of the water, Matt fell onto the ground and rested, chest heaving, his head between his knees.

Then the shots sounded again.

"It sounds like cannon fire," Matt shrieked.

Jay shouted after him, "Whatever you do, don't play that stupid harmonica again!"

Matt stopped short, turned, and pitched the harmonica into the water. Then he threw himself against the flap of the tent and bounced back onto the ground. The tent flap was zipped from the inside.

"Wayne!" he shrieked. "Wayne, open up!"

A loud snore echoed from inside.

Matt and Jay kicked at the tent frame, shouting for Wayne. After what seemed like an eternity, Wayne unzipped the flap and peeked outside. "What?" he muttered.

"What? That's all you can say? Just 'What'?" Matt felt his hands become fists. "You slept through the Civil War! Do you realize you slept through the Civil War? We nearly died out there while you slept the night away!" He wanted to shake Wayne, hard, to make him feel half as frightened as he felt only moments before. "Didn't you see *anything* that happened out there?"

Wayne shook his head. "What?"

Another shot echoed in the dim morning light.

Matt glanced at Jay, who nodded. Without a word, they each lifted an end of Wayne's sleeping bag with him on it and dragged it out into the open air. Despite the battle still raging before them, they dragged Wayne down to the edge of the water and dumped him in with a loud splash. Then, whooping war cries, they ran back into the tent and zipped up the flap.

"Let's get out of here," Jay mumbled, collecting his gear. "I don't know about you, but I'm leaving. Now."

"I'm right behind you," Matt said, picking up remnants of food, a deck of cards, and searching for a pair of dry socks.

"If I live long enough to get home," Jay said. "I'm gonna sleep for two days."

Matt smiled. "I'm never going to sleep again.

With my luck, I'll wake up back in the war."

"We're studying the Civil War next marking period," Jay groaned. "I'm cutting History class until it's over."

"Yeah, but just think how you'll ace the test!" Matt laughed.

Jay smiled. "Yeah."

A loud boom shook the tent.

"What is it?" Jay's voice quivered. "There's got to be a logical explanation. This has gone on long enough. The sun's coming out. Ghosts don't hang around in the daytime, do they?"

"Ghosts hang around anytime and anywhere they want," Matt said solemnly. "We just have to ignore them and go about our business, that's all."

Both boys sat quietly, trembling, keeping their thoughts to themselves. Finally, Jay asked, "You think it's okay to go out there now?"

Matt nodded. "Wayne's out there somewhere. If he's still alive, I'd say it's safe."

Jay hunched his shoulders and frowned. "I don't know. It's starting to feel pretty good right here. I think I'll sit a minute."

"Me too." Matt wrapped his sleeping bag around himself and burrowed down, basking in the rush of warmth that flooded his cold, wet body.

"Right now I'd be pretty happy to see the cops," Jay said.

Matt nodded in agreement.

From just outside the tent, they heard "What . . . ! What the—!"

"It's Wayne," Jay whispered.

Matt shook all over. His knees knocked so violently, he had to hold them. His teeth chattered so hard he almost bit his tongue. "Oh no, don't tell me . . . "

"Hey! You guys! Come here!" Wayne screamed. "Oh no!"

"You go," Jay hissed.

"No, you!" Matt answered.

"I'm staying here."

"Me too."

The sound of marching footsteps echoed across the field into the tent, growing louder and louder every second.

Paralyzed, Jay stared at Matt. "That sounds like the whole army. In fact, it sounds as if they're gonna march right over us. If we don't get out of here, we'll be trampled!"

"Run for it!" Matt screamed. He leaped up and

ripped open the tent flap. Before bolting outside, he craned his neck to see what was going on.

Emerging from a dusty cloud that hung over the trees, four neat lines of young cadets in dress uniforms marched over the water toward them. Their feet never touched the ground or the water. They moved, suspended, in mid-air.

A sudden chill rushed through Matt's heart, and a cold finger crawled up his back and raised the hairs on his neck. He shivered and stared hard at the parade coming toward them, blinking as though he expected them to disappear. Between the neat columns of cadets Confederate soldiers were carrying muskets.

Wayne stood at the edge of the water, shocked by the floating parade that passed right over his head. He turned to stare openmouthed at Matt, who stood behind him and watched the first few ghosts in the parade pass over them into the sky. Matt stood stiffly at attention. He almost wished he could march with them.

"They won!" he shouted. "The Confederate army may have lost the entire Civil War, but they won this battle!"

A column of cadets turned sharply and stopped in front of them, standing at attention.

The marchers all seemed shadowy now, including the soldiers who had served in the battle. The ghosts were proudly answering a silent roll call.

Colonel Bates' voice called out orders clearly and gently. Matt smiled at the sound. He didn't think he would ever forget Alexander Barton wave at him from across the water, then disappear into a cloud.

He scanned the fading line of ghostly soldiers, hoping not to see scary-looking Lieutenant Miles. There was no sign of him.

The ghostly voices became dusty echoes. As suddenly as they had marched into the adjacent field, they disappeared completely into a cloud. The sun blazed out from behind the cloud and made a spotlight on the empty field, its fiery face reflected in the shimmering water.

Suddenly, Matt knew for sure it was all over. They could leave the battlefield safely. The ghosts would not get in their way. They would never see them again.

And that was okay with him.

"They won," Matt whispered. "Colonel Bates must've been so proud."

Without another word, Matt, Wayne, and Jay

folded the tent and collected their gear.

Feeling like the commander of his own tiny army, Matt saluted the battlefield. Then he announced, "On the count of three, men, fall out. One..."

Wayne interrupted, "Can it, Matt. Let's go!"

In single file, they ran through the culvert, scaled the fence with no effort at all, and kept on running till they dropped, chests heaving, on the side of the road.

Smiling with relief, Jay asked, "Do you think they fight here every single night?"

"I don't think so," Matt answered. "Or maybe they do, but only certain people can see them."

"Lucky us," Jay muttered.

"I wonder if they all come back on Halloween," Wayne said hopefully.

Matt looked at Jay and they laughed. Matt answered, "There's only one way to find out."

In unison, all three boys shouted, "No way!"

It's in the Attic

by Cynthia Blair

1

"This place is spooky!" cried Madeline Johnson.

She froze halfway up the creaky wooden staircase that led to the attic. Something about the musty attic at the top of the stairs was making chills run down her spine.

For one thing, it was covered in long, dark shadows. They lay across the huge room, forming eerie shapes. Another thing she noticed was that the air smelled funny, as if no one had been up there in a very long time. And as if *that* weren't bad enough, the corners of the attic were coated with icky cobwebs.

Only a few minutes earlier, Madeline had actually been looking forward to exploring the fourth floor of the big old Victorian house she and her family had just moved into. Yet now that she had a chance to see what it was really like, she was thinking very seriously about turning around and heading right back downstairs.

"Come on," her big brother Brian insisted. He was right behind her, just a few steps below. Like Madeline, he was carrying an empty cardboard carton. "You heard what Mom said. We have to store the extra boxes and all the other stuff that's left over from the move up here.

"Besides," he added in a teasing voice, "you're not afraid of a few ghosts, are you?"

"Ghosts?" Madeline nearly jumped out of her skin. She knew that an eleven-year-old was too grown up to be afraid of ghosts. Yet just hearing the word gave her the creeps.

"Only kidding," said Brian, tugging on the long dark-brown braid that hung down her back. In that same teasing tone, he added, "At least I *think* I am."

Of course he's kidding, Madeline told herself. She paused only a moment longer before carrying her box the rest of the way up. There's no such thing as ghosts. Mom and Dad have been telling me that for years.

Still, as she looked around the dark, shadowy attic, she couldn't help wondering if her parents had been right.

"Where's the light switch?" she asked, looking at her brother over her shoulder.

"The electrical wiring never made it up here," Brian replied. "I'm afraid that whenever you come up into the attic, you'll have to do the old-fashioned thing of bringing in light."

Dropping his box on the floor, he reached into the pocket of his jeans. He pulled out a short round candle and a box of wooden matches.

"We can keep these on this shelf over here." Carefully he lit the wick, then put the candle in the corner. He placed the matches right next to it.

Madeline expected the light from the candle to make the large attic room more comforting. Instead, the flickering flame sent gigantic shadows jumping up onto the walls.

She swallowed hard. "We're done," she announced. "Let's go back downstairs and—"

"Hey, look over here!" Brian was rushing across the attic. Although he was only fourteen, he was already nearly as tall as their father. The wooden floorboards creaked under his weight. "What a great old trunk! I wonder what's in it."

Madeline leaned forward to get a better look at the trunk. As far as she was concerned, it wasn't very interesting. Not only was it covered with dust, it also looked as if it were about to fall apart. To her, it was just one more piece of junk, no different from the boxes and suitcases and broken pieces of furniture like the large oval-shaped mirror with a big crack running through the middle.

But Brian didn't seem to agree. He was kneeling in front of the trunk, examining it as if it were the most fascinating thing in the world.

"There are initials on it, Maddy!" he told her excitedly as he ran his fingers along the front. "'E.S.' Gee, I wonder who E.S. is. Or who E.S. *was*, since this trunk looks like it's at least a hundred years old."

"Who cares?" Madeline said. "Let's just get this job over with as fast as we can. I want to go down to my new room and unpack my doll collection." She folded her arms across her chest, shuddering as she looked around. "Nothing would make me happier than to get away from this creepy attic."

It's in the Attic

Actually, she thought the entire house was creepy. It was so different from the house the Johnsons had lived in before! That house had been modern, two stories high with a two-car garage and a big backyard.

But their new house in Fulton, nearly fifty miles away from her home town, was like something out of a horror story. It was an old-fashioned Victorian mansion with a big porch and fancy trim all over it, built over one hundred fifty years earlier. From the very start, Madeline had thought of it as a place that could never *ever* feel like a real home.

It wasn't only the fact that the house was so old that bothered Madeline. Even more, it was the feeling she'd gotten the first time she'd stepped inside. The long shadowy hallways, the mysterious closets and cupboards built into the walls, the creaky floors that always made her feel as if somebody were sneaking up behind her. . .

Over and over again she'd told herself that sooner or later she'd get used to it. In fact, as she stood in the attic, watching her big brother dust off the trunk with a piece of cloth he'd found tucked away in a corner, she said those very words to herself one more time.

FRIGHT TIME

She still couldn't keep a big fat tear from sliding down her cheek. Quickly she wiped it away. She missed her old home so much she could hardly stand it. She missed her old school, her old friends, her old town . . .

"Good news! I just found the silverware!" her mother suddenly called up the stairs.

"Great!" Brian called down. "Tonight we can have dinner without plastic forks! Not that it wasn't kind of fun, having a picnic in the middle of October . . ."

Madeline laughed. But she still didn't feel much better.

Mrs. Johnson came up the stairs, carrying another empty cardboard carton. "We might as well keep this box up here with all the others," she said cheerfully.

Once she'd reached the top of the stairs, she looked around. "Isn't this attic wonderful?" she asked. "It's one of my favorite parts of the house. In fact, when the real estate agent first showed it to us, I turned to Daddy and said, 'My mind is made up. This is the house for us!'"

Just like her son and her daughter, Mrs. Johnson was dressed in a pair of jeans and an old sweatshirt. There was a big smudge on her face. Her hair, the same dark brown as both Madeline's and Brian's, was pulled back into a pony tail.

"When you're finished up here," Mrs. Johnson said, "I could use some help downstairs. Now that I've found all our plates and cups and silverware, I have to wash them off and put them in the cabinets."

"If you're looking for a volunteer," Madeline offered, "you just found one."

"It seems Maddy isn't exactly crazy about the attic," Brian said. He took the box from his mother and added it to the pile in the corner. "I'll finish up here. Why don't you go help Mom?"

"That would be fine," said Mrs. Johnson. "But I also have another job for you, Brian. Would you please pick up some shelf paper to line the kitchen cabinets?"

"At your service." Brian brushed the dust off his hands and dashed off.

"Goodness," Mrs. Johnson commented as she went down the stairs a few minutes later, "moving to a new house is a big job."

"If it were up to me," Madeline muttered, "we would have stayed where we were."

"New things only seem new for a little while. Before long, they start to feel just as familiar as old things."

Madeline looked up at her mother and saw the warmth in her eyes. She knew she was trying hard to make her feel better.

They went down two more flights of creaking stairs. They reached the first floor, passing through the big front parlor with its stone fireplace, through the huge dining room, into the kitchen.

Madeline saw how old the cabinets were—just like everything else in the house. Lining them with paper was a good idea.

The first two boxes of dishes had barely been unpacked when the back door flew open. Brian burst inside, a brown paper bag under his arm.

"Did you get the shelf paper?" Mrs. Johnson asked.

"Exactly what you asked for." Brian was out of breath. "But I got something else, too—something even better!"

He sat down at the kitchen table, and he leaned forward. He kept his eyes focused on his sister. "I found out the truth about this house."

"What are you talking about?" asked Mrs. Johnson.

"It's almost impossible to believe," Brian said. "But everyone says it's true. The man who owns the hardware store, the woman who runs the bakery next door—"

"Tell us," Madeline demanded. "Brian, what did you find out?"

Her brother leaned back in his chair, a strange smile on his face. "Mom, Madeline, this house is *haunted!*"

"Haunted!" Mrs. Johnson exclaimed. "What are you talking about?"

"It's true, Mom," Brian insisted. "I told you it was hard to believe."

Mrs. Johnson sat down at the kitchen table. "Maybe you'd better go back to the beginning."

"Once upon a time," Brian began in a low voice, "over a hundred years ago, a beautiful young woman named Emily Simms lived in this house with her parents. When she was twenty years old, she fell in love with a man named Charles Day. They were supposed to get married.

"On her wedding day, Emily got dressed in her bridal gown, put on her long white veil, and went to the church with her family and her friends. The organist kept playing as everyone waited—"

"What were they waiting for?" asked Madeline, suddenly interested.

"Charles. He was late." Brian paused to take a deep breath. "In fact, he never showed up at all. He left Emily standing at the altar . . . *alone*."

"What a sad story!" Mrs. Johnson said.

"You haven't even heard the saddest part," said Brian. "Emily Simms never got over it. She loved Charles so much that she never stopped believing that one day he'd come for her. She spent the rest of her life waiting for him."

"You mean she never married Charles?" asked Mrs. Johnson.

Brian shook his head. "Not Charles or anybody else. She lived to be eighty years old, yet never again did she leave her home. And according to the people in town, she's still here. They say she hasn't stopped waiting for Charles."

A shiver ran down Madeline's spine as her brother looked first at her, then at her mother. In a voice so soft she could barely hear him, he said, "In other words, the ghost of Emily Simms lives in this house!"

IT'S IN THE ATTIC

2

That night, as she lay in bed, Madeline couldn't stop thinking about the story her brother had told. A ghost right here in this house? It was impossible! Everybody knew there was no such thing as ghosts!

Still, she had to admit that this old house *did* feel strange. She'd decided that even before she'd ever heard of Emily Simms. The creaky floorboards, the shadowy hallways, the strange feeling she got every now and then that someone— or *something*—was behind her...

It was a long time before she drifted off to sleep. And even though she didn't really believe in ghosts, she kept the blankets pulled way up to her chin.

By early the next morning, she'd forgotten all about her brother's story. She was too busy thinking about the day ahead, her very first day at a brand new school.

Madeline's heart beat quickly as she walked from the bus to the front door of the new school. All around her children swarmed into the building. Yet never before in her life had she felt so alone.

How strange it felt to see so many faces, but not recognize a single one! As she made her way toward Ms. Bradley's sixth grade classroom, she was certain she'd never make a single friend here.

At least her teacher seemed nice. She greeted Madeline as she came in, showing her to a seat in front of the room.

"Don't worry, Madeline," Ms. Bradley whispered. "I know it's hard to start out at a new school. But before you know it, you'll know everyone in your class. Soon you won't feel like the 'new girl' at all."

Turning to the class, she said, "I'd like to introduce a new student. Madeline Johnson just moved here from Willowbrook. I hope you'll all do your best to make her feel welcome."

Most of the class turned to get a better look at Madeline. She could feel her cheeks turning red. She pretended to be very interested in the pencil on her desk. She studied it as if it were something she'd never seen before.

"Before we get started with today's spelling lesson," Mrs. Bradley went on, "we have a special assignment. Your homework for tonight is to memorize a poem. Over the next few days, each of you will stand up in front of the class and recite it.

It's in the Attic

I'll use the school's video camera to tape you so you can see for yourselves how well you do."

The boy sitting next to Madeline, short and stocky with straight brown hair and a face full of freckles, groaned loudly.

"I have a feeling this will be more fun than you expect, Tommy," said Mrs. Bradley. "Now who wants to write this week's spelling words on the board?"

Madeline was glad that the teacher kept them busy all morning. She was much happier doing math problems and spelling words than talking to the other students. She still couldn't keep their names straight, no matter how hard she tried. And every once in a while she looked up and saw that someone was staring at her.

At lunch, she sat down at the first table she came to. At the other end were two girls she recognized from her class. She kept her eyes down as she ate, wishing she could think of something to say to them.

She was glad that one of them finally spoke. "Mrs. Bradley said you come from Willowbrook," the taller one said. She had long straight hair, a pretty shade of light brown.

Madeline nodded.

"I've been there," the girl said. "Isn't there a big park on the edge of town?"

"That's right," said Madeline. "It has a wonderful playground and a pond and a bicycle path that goes on for miles."

She swallowed hard. Tears had filled her eyes. The last thing she wanted was for these girls to think she was a crybaby. Still, just talking about Willowbrook Park was making her homesick.

I'll *never* get used to this place! she thought as she took another bite of her sandwich. Never in a million years!

"We have a nice park here in Fulton, too," the other girl said. She had blond curly hair and the bluest eyes Madeline had ever seen. "It has a great bike path, too."

"And a terrific jungle gym!" said the brown-haired girl. "You can climb as high as a building." She took a sip from her carton of milk before adding, "By the way, my name is Catherine. This is Vicky. We've been friends since kindergarten."

Madeline couldn't believe it. She was actually having fun talking to these girls.

"Where do you live?" asked Vicky.

"The big old Victorian on the corner of Elm and Crescent."

It's in the Attic

All of a sudden Catherine's eyes grew wide. She froze, holding her carton of milk in mid-air. "You're kidding."

"No," said Madeline. "My family and I moved into that house a few days ago."

Catherine and Vicky looked at each other. Vicky was wearing the same shocked expression as Catherine.

Madeline swallowed hard. "What's wrong?" she asked in a soft voice.

"Nothing," Vicky replied quickly. "It's just that ... "

"We knew the girl who lived there right before you," Catherine chimed in. "Her name was Ann Wilson. We were just starting to become friends when ... when she disappeared."

"Disappeared?" Madeline repeated. Her mouth had suddenly gotten very dry. She sat without moving, feeling as if the room around her were fading away.

Vicky nodded. Her blue eyes were big and round. "It was the strangest thing," she said. "Nobody ever really understood what happened. All we know is that after the Wilsons had been living in that house for less than two weeks, the entire family packed up and left in the middle of the night!"

"That's right," said Catherine. "And they never set foot in Fulton again!"

3

Even though her conversation with Catherine and Vicky left Madeline with a terrible feeling in the pit of her stomach, she didn't tell her family what she'd heard about the mysterious disappearance of the house's former owners.

"The whole thing is ridiculous," she muttered to herself as she set the table for dinner that evening. "Nothing but rumors—rumors as silly as Brian's ghost story! The Wilsons probably had a perfectly good reason for moving out. Maybe the house was just too big or old or too cold or too expensive . . ."

Still, she couldn't get rid of that uneasy feeling—the feeling that something wasn't quite right. She decided to forget all the stories she was hearing about the house.

But it wasn't going to be quite that simple.

"I heard her," Brian said over dinner that

night, his eyes narrowing. "Last night, I heard the ghost of Emily Simms."

Madeline felt the knot in her stomach grow tighter.

"Ghost?" repeated Mr. Johnson. "What ghost?"

"Surely you're not serious," said Mrs. Johnson to her son.

"I'm dead serious," said Brian. "I woke up in the middle of the night. My room was completely dark. Everything was quiet. At first I couldn't figure out what woke me up. And then I heard it. A woman's voice, *crying*."

"She was crying?" Mrs. Johnson asked. "Poor Emily!"

"Poor Emily!" Mr. Johnson laughed. "You're talking about a ghost as if she were real!"

"She *is* real," Brian insisted. "And hearing her last night has made me really curious."

"I don't believe in ghosts, of course," said Mrs. Johnson, "but it might be interesting to learn about the people who lived here before us. Why don't you and Maddy go up to the attic after dinner and poke around?"

"Next stop, the attic!" cried Brian. "Sis, you and I have a date."

"Oh, no, you don't!" Madeline shook her head firmly. "You're not getting me up into that creepy old attic again!"

"Don't worry." Brian reached over and patted her hand. "No matter what happens, your big brother will be there to protect you."

I can't believe I let myself be talked into this, Madeline thought as she followed Brian up the stairs later that evening. Right now, the last place I feel like spending a cold, dark night is a dirty old attic.

Madeline told herself over and over again that it was the dust and the cobwebs that made her dislike the attic so much.

Once they'd lit the candle, Brian headed straight for the trunk in the corner, the one with "E.S." on the lid. Madeline made a point of looking the other way. She stood in front of the cracked mirror, running her finger along the wooden frame.

"I wonder if Mom would let me put this in my room," she mumbled. "Maybe if I painted it—"

"Hey, look at this!" her brother suddenly cried. He reached inside the trunk and pulled out something long and white.

"What is it?" Madeline's heart began to pound

as she squinted in the dim light of the candle.

"I'm not sure." Brian held it out to get a better look. It was a long piece of fabric, made entirely of lace. Even though it was so old it was torn at the ends, it was still beautiful.

"I think it's a veil," she told him. "You know, what brides wear."

"I guess it belonged to Emily. Do you want it?"

Madeline shook her head. "No thanks," she said firmly.

"Wait. There's more stuff in here." Brian stuck his head into the trunk. "A bunch of old clothes, mostly. Nothing as fancy as that veil. But here's something that's kind of pretty."

He reached inside once again. This time he pulled out a white lace handkerchief. Embroidered in one corner in fine pink thread were the initials "E.S."

Though Madeline had decided she'd be better off having as little to do with Emily Simms as possible, something about the handkerchief intrigued her.

"Let me see that." Madeline took the handkerchief from him, anxious to get a better look.

Nothing prepared her for the chills that ran down her spine the moment she touched it. She suddenly had the strangest feeling. It was almost as if someone else were right there in the room with them.

She whirled around, expecting to find someone behind her. No one was there.

"Here. Take this silly thing back." Madeline threw the handkerchief into the trunk. "As a matter of fact, we'd probably be better off if we just threw out all this junk."

Brian didn't seem aware that anything out of the ordinary had happened. He moved the handkerchief into the corner of the trunk, then slammed the lid shut. "I have a better idea," he said. "Let's give Mom the chance to look through all this old stuff. I bet she'd enjoy it. I'll bring the whole trunk downstairs. You don't mind if I stick it in your room, do you?"

"*My* room!" Madeline cried.

"Just for a few days. That way, Mom won't have to come all the way up here to go through all these clothes. Besides, the light downstairs is much better."

Madeline swallowed hard. "I—I'd rather leave it up here."

But Brian had already moved away to the back corner of the attic. "Wow! Hey, Maddy! Look at *this*!"

He reached into the shadows and brought out something Madeline could see was a wedding dress. The lacy fabric was yellowing with age and the sleeves were tattered. Even so, she could see that it had once been beautiful.

"Here, Maddy," Brian said, holding it out to her. "Why don't you try it on?"

"Are you nuts?" Madeline jumped backwards. "First of all, that old dress is so dusty I don't even want to touch it. Second of all, why would I want to put on somebody else's old wedding dress?"

Before Brian had a chance to answer, Mrs. Johnson called to them from downstairs.

"I know you're having fun up there," she said, "but Maddy's favorite television show is about to start."

"Thanks for reminding me," Madeline yelled back down. Looking at her brother, she added, "And I don't intend to miss it—not for Emily Simms or anyone else!"

Brian was already picking up the heavy trunk. "Since our own personal ghost doesn't scare you, storing this in your room shouldn't bother you at all."

Madeline didn't waste her time protesting. Instead, she hurried down the stairs. She didn't want to admit it to Brian, but for some reason it was impossible to stay in the attic a moment longer.

The television show was funny. At least Mrs. Johnson kept laughing. Maddy sat on the couch next to her, completely silent. No matter how hard she tried, she couldn't pay attention. She kept thinking about the attic. She kept picturing Emily's wedding dress and her veil and the other things in the trunk. Most of all, she couldn't stop remembering the odd way she'd felt when she'd touched that handkerchief.

"I'm going up to bed," she finally announced.

Her mother looked surprised. "But the show's not over."

"I know. I'm pretty tired, though. Going to a new school for the first time is hard work."

"I can imagine," her mother replied, smiling. "Good night, honey. See you in the morning."

Madeline really was tired, and she'd planned to go straight to bed. But when she reached her bedroom, she paused only for a moment. Even before she knew what was happening, she found herself passing it by and instead heading for the staircase. Slowly she began to climb upstairs, not understanding why she was going up to the attic, yet never once thinking about turning back. It was as if some irresistible force were pulling her up.

In the attic, Madeline lit the candle and headed straight for the wedding dress. In the pale light of the flickering flame, she quickly pulled the dress on, right over her tee-shirt and jeans. Standing in front of the cracked mirror, she barely recognized her reflection.

Her heart skipped a beat. Not only did she look different, Madeline suddenly *felt* different. She felt lighter, yet at the same time very sad. It was as if something were tearing at her, something terrible, something she couldn't forget.... She closed her eyes. It was as if she were somebody else. Her thoughts were beginning to feel far away. And her mind was clouded. It was almost as if she were drifting off to some other place....

"I thought I heard somebody up here!"

Madeline's eyes snapped open as Brian's voice cut through the dreamy state she had drifted into. She whirled around and saw her brother standing right behind her, grinning.

"At first I thought a squirrel had gotten into

the attic. But now I see you couldn't resist trying on poor old Emily's wedding dress after all!"

"Don't call her that!" Madeline cried. The sharp tone of her voice surprised her. Quickly she pulled off the dress. "I—I just wanted to see if it fit."

"Oh, it fits, all right," said Brian. "If you ask me, it looks like you and Emily are practically the same size."

"Are you kidding? This dress is much too big for me." She threw it down on the trunk. "Now if you'll excuse me, I'm going to bed."

"Good-night," Brian called after her. "Sweet dreams—about Emily Simms, of course!"

Madeline wanted to forget all about Emily and the attic and the wedding dress. But as she went into her bedroom, the first thing she spotted was the trunk.

She looked at her bed, reminding herself that it was getting late and that she was tired. She really meant to put on her nightgown and climb in underneath the blankets, but she instead went over to the trunk and knelt down in front of it.

Slowly she lifted the heavy lid. Her heart was pounding and her hands were trembling as one by one, she took out the clothing folded up neatly inside. A velvet dress, a fringed shawl, a ruffled blouse. . . . As she touched each one, that same peculiar feeling came over her. And as soon as she let go, the feeling went away and she went back to being Madeline Johnson again.

Finally the trunk was empty. She was about to pile everything back inside when something else caught her eye. Lying at the very bottom was a pale pink envelope. The sight of it made her heart beat.

Madeline stared at it for a very long time. Finally, she picked it up. As she held it, she saw that printed on the back of the fine stationery, in very fancy lettering, was the letter "S."

" 'S,' " she said aloud. " 'S' is for Simms."

With trembling hands she opened the envelope to take out the letter folded up inside. But before she had a chance, she felt cold, dry, wrinkled fingers close around her wrist.

4

"No!" Madeline screamed, pulling her hand away.

Yet when she turned to look, there was no one

there. She saw nothing.

"But she's here!" she whispered, a wave of terror rushing over her. "She's here! She's in the room with me!"

Yet as she sat frozen to the spot, unable to move, she felt her fear slip away. The feeling that someone else was near—someone she couldn't see or hear—faded. She was alone.

Madeline's heart was pounding so hard her head throbbed. Looking down, she saw the envelope lying on the floor, where it had fallen when she'd screamed. She hesitated for a few seconds before finally reaching down and picking it up.

This time, when she took the letter out of its envelope, she felt nothing. She had just unfolded it and was about to begin reading when she heard someone come into her room.

"Hi, Brian," she said casually, glancing up to see her brother standing in the doorway.

"What have you got there?" he asked, pointing at the letter.

"Oh . . . nothing." Madeline tossed it onto the bed in front of her. "Just some old letters I was looking through."

"Bor-ing." Brian was already turning away.

It's in the Attic

"I've got to study. Math quiz tomorrow."

Madeline felt bad about holding back from her brother. Usually she told him everything. But this was something new that she didn't want to share with anyone else, something she couldn't explain.

When she heard Brian close his bedroom door, she picked up the letter. Taking a deep breath, she began to read.

"My dear sister," the letter began. "I am writing to tell you how worried I am about my daughter Emily. She has not left the house in weeks. Instead she spends her days upstairs in the attic, standing in front of the mirror in her wedding dress.

"Although it made my heart ache, I kept wondering if was possible poor Emily is still waiting for Charles. It took all my courage, but I finally asked her why she no longer walked in the garden or visited with her friends. 'Why do you spend your days roaming the attic?' I asked, 'wearing your wedding gown?'

"Dear sister," Emily's mother went on, "my worst fears were realized. My daughter turned to me, her eyes filled with sadness. She said, 'I will never rest until I find out whether or not

Charles really loved me.'

"I have tried to contact Charles' parents," the letter went on. "But while I have written to them again and again, my letters have all gone unanswered. You know that they never approved of the match, and so I am not surprised by their silence. Still, it is so hard for me, watching my poor Emily, seeing how badly her young heart is broken.

"How I wish I could help her! Yet I fear there is nothing to do but wait, never giving up hope that one day she will leave her pain behind. . . . "

It took Madeline a long time to fall asleep that night. Even after she'd turned out the lights, she lay in bed, tossing and turning, thinking about Emily. She couldn't stop picturing her in her mind. She saw Emily standing in the attic just as she herself had, wearing the same dress, looking into the same mirror. Suddenly she *knew* Emily Simms. Even more, it was almost as if Emily were *part* of her.

Something in the room felt different.

And then she heard it. It was quiet at first, so soft she could barely hear it. But quickly the sound grew louder. It surrounded her, as if the very walls of the house were stricken with sadness. Terrible, heartbreaking crying that at the same time made her blood run cold.

And then it stopped, as suddenly as it had begun. A silence almost as terrifying as the sobbing hung over the room.

Slowly, Madeline climbed out of bed, her long nightgown flowing behind her. She stood in the middle of her room, all her tiredness gone. She was wide awake. Her heart was pounding, sending blood rushing through her so hard it made her dizzy.

"Emily?" she said, her voice a hoarse whisper. Her head throbbed. "Are you here?"

Her words were met with nothing but the stifling silence.

It wasn't until she reached the trunk that Madeline realized that was where she'd been headed all along. The moonlight shone straight through the window, lighting up the trunk as if it were in a spotlight.

For a long time she stood in front of it, afraid to look down. Yet she knew she must.

She swallowed hard. And then she lowered her eyes toward the lid of the dusty wooden trunk.

Written in the dust were the words, "I love

you so, Charles." Lying nearby, on top of the trunk, was the lace handkerchief.

Madeline cried out. Without knowing what she was about to do, she grabbed the handkerchief and clutched it to her heart. The last thing she remembered before falling to the floor was the feeling of her own fingers as they touched her throat: dry, wrinkled, and icy cold.

5

"What on *earth*—?"

Madeline was dragged out of a deep sleep by the sound of her brother's voice. Brian was talking to her, but she couldn't make sense of his words.

"Are you all right?" he demanded. "Maddy, what happened? What's going on?"

When she opened her eyes, Madeline still didn't understand where she was. She blinked hard a few times. Slowly she saw that she was in her own bedroom, but that she was lying on the floor, near the trunk.

"I guess I fell asleep," she muttered, trying to pull herself up.

It's in the Attic

Her arms and legs felt so heavy she could scarcely move. Sitting up was a struggle. When she finally managed it, she almost wished she hadn't.

"Oh, my gosh!" she cried. "What have I done?"

Lying on the floor next to her was one of the dolls from her special collection, an antique bride doll that had always been one of her favorites. The doll's beautiful lace dress had been ripped into tiny pieces that lay thrown all around. Madeline stared at the mess in astonishment.

Brian knelt down on the floor beside her. He put his arms around his sister's shoulders and hugged her. "Maddy, I don't understand this. There's something going on here—"

"I loved this doll." Sadly she picked up a piece of the dress. "I—I just don't know what came over me."

"Maddy, listen to me." Brian gripped her shoulders more tightly. "Let me help you. There's something happening here—something we can't understand. We have to tell Mom and Dad—"

"No!" Madeline cried. "Please, Brian. Don't tell them!"

"Maddy, I've got to." His voice was hoarse. "Something terrible is in this house!"

159

She stared at the doll, surrounded by bits of shredded fabric. "Don't tell them yet. *Please!*"

Brian stared at her for a long time. Finally, he said, "All right, Maddy. If you're sure."

She just nodded. She couldn't explain it—not to Brian, not even to herself—but Madeline was certain that whatever was happening was strictly between Emily Simms and herself.

She was the one Emily had chosen . . . and there was no one else who could help.

Madeline felt as if she were in a daze as she sat at her desk later that morning. When her teacher asked for someone to volunteer to be the first to recite the required poem, she slumped down lower in her seat.

A feeling of dread washed over her as she heard Ms. Bradley say, "Madeline? Would you like to start?"

Madeline dragged herself up out of her seat. As she stood in front of the classroom, her heart was pounding. She looked at the other members of her class, all staring at her expectantly.

She took a deep breath, struggling to remember the opening lines of the poem she had memorized for the assignment, "Stopping By Woods on a Snowy Evening" by Robert Frost. The first words quickly popped into her mind. "Whose woods these are, I think I know...."

She opened her mouth, ready to start. Yet before she had gotten more than the first four or five words out, a wave of dizziness suddenly swept over her. Madeline closed her eyes. She grabbed hold of Ms. Bradley's desk as she felt herself sway from side to side. The bulletin boards at the back of the classroom, the faces of the other students, the desks and chairs . . . they grew hazy, fading further and further away. She struggled desperately to take deep breaths. But she could feel herself drifting....

When her eyes snapped open, Madeline didn't know how much time had passed. She was still standing in front of the classroom, staring at the same bulletin boards and the same sea of faces. Yet this time, her classmates looked astonished.

"Wh—what happened?" she muttered.

She blinked hard a few times. Ms. Bradley was crossing the room toward her. Like everyone else, she looked confused.

"Madeline, is this some kind of joke?" the teacher asked.

"No, I . . . " Madeline let her voice trail off. She

had no idea what had just happened. Yet from the expressions on everyone's faces, it had been something extraordinary.

"Perhaps you can explain," said Ms. Bradley. "Let me play the videotape for you."

Madeline went back to her seat. She could feel the eyes of her classmates burning into her.

Ms. Bradley switched on the television. After a few seconds, Madeline saw herself on the screen.

Her heart pounded fiercely as she watched herself say the first words of the poem. Then the girl on the television screen stopped talking. She closed her eyes and grabbed hold of the edge of Ms. Bradley's desk. It was happening exactly the way she remembered it.

Yet she had no memory at all of what she saw next.

Horrified, Madeline watched herself change before her very eyes. The expression on her face, the way she was standing, even her voice.

"Charles," she was saying. Her voice was odd, deep and dramatic. She even pronounced her words differently. "Charles, how could you ever have done this to me? I've waited for you so long. I'm still waiting . . ."

And then the girl on the television screen

opened her eyes. Madeline clearly remembered what had happened from that point on. Now, it all made sense. And yet, it made no sense at all!

Ms. Bradley snapped off the television.

"Perhaps you'd like to try again tomorrow," Ms. Bradley said. "Sarah, why don't you take your turn next?"

For the rest of the morning, Madeline found it impossible to listen. One by one, her classmates got up to recite their poems. But her thoughts were far away. Emily had taken over her thinking.

Ever since she'd first touched Emily's handkerchief, she knew that there was a connection between her and the woman who'd lived in her house nearly a hundred years earlier. Now she could see there was much more than just a connection. Brian had been right. Something *was* happening.

Slowly but surely, Madeline was *becoming* Emily Simms.

At lunch, Madeline made a point of choosing a corner table. She hoped she'd be able to sit by herself. But before long she saw Vicky and Catherine heading in her direction, carrying their trays.

"It was the ghost, wasn't it?" Vicky asked

breathlessly, dropping into the seat opposite her. "It was Emily!"

"She's becoming part of you!" Catherine cried. "I wonder if that's also what happened to Ann Wilson—"

"No!" Madeline insisted. "I was just . . . showing off, that's all. I got so nervous standing up there that I forgot the whole stupid poem I'd tried to memorize. I decided to kid around a little, instead."

Vicky and Catherine looked at each other. Madeline could tell by the expressions on their faces that they weren't quite sure whether to believe her or not.

She was about to insist again that the scene in the classroom had been nothing more than her attempt at being funny when she heard someone behind her moan, "Ooo-o-o-oh!"

She whirled around. Just as she'd expected, she found Tommy, the boy from her class, standing there, making an ugly face. A friend of his, Dan, was right behind him.

"I'm a ghost!" cried Tommy. "I live in that creepy old house on the corner of Elm and Crescent. Oh, Charles, I miss you so! Ooo-o-o-oh!"

Madeline just stared at him, so furious she

164

could hardly talk.

"The ghost of Emily Simms is *real!*" Catherine finally cried.

"Sure she is," Tommy shot back. "And I'm Elvis Presley!" He cracked up at his own joke.

"Come on," Dan said. "You don't really think anybody will believe that dumb story about your house being haunted, do you?"

"*I* believe it," Catherine insisted.

"Me, too," Vicky seconded.

"You do?" Dan looked strangely at both girls.

Catherine nodded. "This isn't the first time I've heard that story. A lot of people in town believe that the ghost of Emily Simms still lives in the house that Madeline and her family moved into. Remember what happened to the Wilsons? I've been hearing about that ghost practically my whole life."

"Me, too," her friend Vicky joined in. "I remember the first time I heard about Emily Simms. It was Halloween, and my older sister told me the story. I was so scared I couldn't fall asleep for hours!"

"A ghost, huh?" Tommy folded his arms across his chest.

Vicky nodded. "I'm positive that Emily

Simms' ghost took possession of Madeline's body today while she was reciting that poem."

Madeline started to protest, but Catherine grabbed her arm. "Do you think maybe I could come over some time and see your house?"

"Oh, please!" Vicky cried. "I want to see it, too." Suddenly her eyes grew wide. "Maybe if we're lucky we'll actually *see* Emily's ghost!"

"Can we, please?" said Catherine. "Could Vicky and I come over?"

Madeline swallowed hard. "Sure," she said. "If you really want to."

She knew she should have been glad these two girls wanted to come over. Yet as she told them they could, a terrible sense of dread suddenly came over her. She couldn't explain it, but she suddenly had the feeling that Emily Simms would be angry if she let strangers into her house.

And making the ghost angry, she suspected, could turn out to be very, very dangerous.

6

"Mom," Madeline said over dinner that evening, "today two girls at school asked if they could come over after school one day. Would that be okay?"

"How nice!" Mrs. Johnson exclaimed. "Of course, Maddy. I'm glad you're making new friends."

"Your mother and I have been worried about you," Mr. Johnson added. "We know how hard it must be, moving to a new town and starting at a new school."

"Thank goodness you're not all wrapped up in that silly idea about a ghost living here anymore!" Mrs. Johnson cried.

Brian cast his sister a knowing look. But neither of them said a word.

"As far as I'm concerned," their mother went on, "I'd be happy if I never heard another word about that ridiculous ghost. What are your new friends' names?"

"Catherine and Vicky," said Madeline.

"I'll stop off at the bakery in town and get some cookies," said Mrs. Johnson. "Having new friends over for the first time is a very special occasion."

Madeline just nodded. It was just as well that Brian barged into the conversation just then. Talk turned to the upcoming try-outs for his school's basketball team. Madeline pretended to be listening, but as she sat with her chin resting in her hands, her mind wandered. As was more and more the case lately, she was much happier thinking about Emily, leaving the real world far behind.

"Madeline," Mrs. Johnson called upstairs later that same evening. "It's nine o'clock. Time to get ready for bed!"

"Okay, Mom. I just have to finish some homework."

She'd been lying across her bed for almost an hour, staring at the problems in her math book. She couldn't concentrate on schoolwork. As a matter of fact, no matter how hard she tried, she found it impossible to concentrate on *anything* besides Emily Simms.

Suddenly she slammed her math book shut. She knew she wasn't going to get any work done. At least, not yet. Not before she finished doing something much more important.

Slowly Madeline climbed off her bed and tiptoed across the floor, down the hall and up the stairs, closer and closer to the attic.

It was hard to believe that only two days earlier she'd actually been afraid of coming up here. Now she was so drawn to this place that she couldn't keep away. Although she couldn't explain it, she felt as if she belonged up there. She struck a wooden match and lit the candle on the shelf. Huge shadows leaped onto the walls. They moved slowly in the flame's flickering light, changing shape, changing size. The sounds of her family, moving around downstairs, seemed very far away. Soon she forgot they were even in the house. She was too busy slipping on Emily's wedding dress.

She stood in front of the mirror, staring at her reflection. How beautiful the dress was! She hadn't really looked at it closely before. The skirt was full, made of yards and yards of fabric. The neckline was so pretty, the lace that trimmed the sleeves so fragile it looked as if it might crumble in her hands.

And then, suddenly, the reflection in the mirror faded. All around her, the attic began to spin. That strange sensation she'd experienced before was overcoming her.

The feeling was frightening. It was like being lost, like being taken away. Yet at the same time, something inside her longed to give in to it.

She closed her eyes and let it sweep over her.

FRIGHT TIME

There was a feeling of lightness, as though she was no longer connected to her body. But she was gripped with sadness. Her heart was heavy with a sorrow unlike any she'd ever known before.

What was more frightening even, she no longer felt like Madeline Johnson. Instead, she felt as if she were someone else.

Slowly she became aware of soft music in the distance. The sweet, tinkling sound reminded her of a music box.

Madeline recognized the song right away. "Here comes the bride, all dressed in white . . ." It was the famous Wedding March that many a bride had heard playing in the background as she walked down the aisle to marry the man she loved.

The music grew louder and louder. But as it filled the attic, it no longer sounded sweet. Instead it became rough and harsh. Madeline covered her ears, desperate to block out the terrible sound.

And then another sound broke in. Madeline's heart ached as over the sound of the music she heard a woman sobbing. It was the saddest thing she'd ever heard. The woman was crying as if her heart were breaking.

"Emily!" Madeline cried, reaching outward with both arms. Tears streamed down her cheeks. It was as if the sadness that filled the room were her own. "Emily, don't cry! Let me help you, please!"

A terrible iciness chilled the room. Madeline shuddered.

And then, suddenly, a chill even worse than the coldness that surrounded her ran down her spine.

"Come to me!" she heard a woman's voice whisper. "I don't want to be alone!"

From out of the shadows emerged a pale form. It was the outline of a woman, dressed in white. Madeline stood frozen to the spot, too terrified to move.

And then a rush of cold air swept through the attic. The candle she'd lit flickered and died. As the pale figure came closer, reaching to touch her with her thin, wrinkled hand, Madeline screamed.

7

"She was there in the attic with me!" Madeline cried, her heart still pounding like a jackhammer. "I *saw* her, Brian! I saw her . . . and I heard her. She spoke to me!"

She rushed into her brother's room after racing down the attic stairs, the image of Emily Simms's ghost still burning into her brain.

"What does she want?" Brian demanded.

"I—I'm not sure." She realized she was shaking all over as she sank onto his bed. "I was so scared, Brian! All I can remember is that she said something about not wanting to be alone."

She thought for a few seconds, then shook her head. "I'm afraid of the ghost, Brian, but at the same time I feel sorry for her. It's almost as if she needs me."

"But Maddy!" Brian said. "Emily Simms is dead! What could she possibly need from you, or from anybody else?"

Before she had a chance to answer, he went on. "Look, Maddy. You've got to try to forget about all this. Going up into the attic, touching Emily's things. The way you're acting is making me nervous. You'd be much better off spending your time making friends and getting used to your new school than hanging around with a ghost."

Madeline just nodded. She didn't bother to explain that she wasn't the one responsible. What was going on between her and Emily Simms was something that was completely out of her control.

At school the following day, Madeline found it difficult to listen to Ms. Bradley. She kept thinking about Emily, and what it had been like to be in the same room as a ghost. It was all she could do to keep from telling everyone she saw about the experience.

As the day drew to a close, she forced herself to think about Vicky and Catherine, who were coming over that afternoon. Maybe it wouldn't hurt to tell them, she decided. After all, they believed the ghost of Emily Simms was real. And they were curious to know what had happened to their friend Ann Wilson and her family.

She waited until after school, when they were all riding home on the schoolbus and nobody else was around.

"You'll never guess what happened to me last night," she told them, her voice a whisper. "I saw Emily Simms!"

She watched as Vicky and Catherine's eyes grew wide. Encouraged by how interested they were, she began to tell them the whole story.

As the schoolbus turned onto her street, she finished by saying, "Being in the attic with a real ghost last night was the scariest thing that's ever happened to me!"

"Oh, Maddy! You're so lucky!" Vicky said with a sigh.

"Lucky?" Madeline repeated, astonished.

Vicky nodded. "Imagine, meeting up with a real ghost!"

"Do you think *we'll* be able to hear Emily's wedding music?" asked Catherine.

"I-I'm not sure," Madeline replied. She still wasn't certain she'd done the right thing in telling them. After thinking for a few seconds, she added, "But I guess it wouldn't hurt to show you her wedding dress."

"Can we try it on?" Catherine's eyes were open wide.

"No!" Madeline cried. "I don't think that'd be a good idea." Not wanting to sound selfish, she added, "It's very old. I wouldn't want it to tear."

"Come on, Madeline," Vicky insisted. "We'll be careful. I promise!"

The very idea of letting them try on Emily's wedding dress made her uneasy. She wondered if letting them in on her secret had been a mistake.

"We'll have to ask my mom," she finally said. She could only hope her mother would back her up.

When the three girls burst into the kitchen and found Mrs. Johnson mixing hot chocolate on the stove, Emily Simms' wedding dress was long forgotten.

"There's a chill in the air today," said Madeline's mother. "I thought you girls might like something warm to drink. And I stopped off at the bakery on my way home from work and picked up some cookies."

As Madeline introduced her two new friends to her mother, she was struck by the fact that for the first time since she'd moved, she felt happy. On this crisp fall afternoon, the house felt so cozy. The smell of the hot chocolate, the big plate of cookies on the table, the good feeling that came from sitting in the kitchen with two girls she really liked, talking and laughing and having fun. She was actually starting to feel at home.

"When can we see the attic?" Vicky finally asked, popping the last of a cookie into her mouth.

"I want to see everything," Catherine added. "The trunk, the handkerchief—"

"And I want to try on that wedding dress," said Vicky.

"Mom," Madeline said slowly, "don't you think that old dress is too fragile? I wouldn't want anything to happen to it."

"I think it'll be all right," said Mrs. Johnson. "Just be careful."

Be careful. Those words echoed through Madeline's head as she headed up the stairs toward her bedroom. Behind her, Vicky and Catherine chattered away excitedly about how much they hoped they'd meet up with the ghost.

As the three girls reached the second floor, Vicky commented, "This is a great house! You're so lucky, Maddy."

"It must be so much fun living here," Catherine agreed with a sigh. "My family lives in an ordinary house. It's nice and all that, but we don't have long hallways and creaky staircases and mysterious attics. And we certainly don't have our own ghost!"

When they'd reached Madeline's room, she led them over to the corner. "This is Emily's trunk." She pointed to the words written in the dust. "See? These are the words she wrote. And here's the handkerchief she left behind. Everything is still exactly where I found it."

"Wow," said Catherine, her voice filled with

awe. "Imagine, a real live ghost!"

"Look at that handkerchief!" Vicky exclaimed. "It looks so old!"

"Can we see the attic now?" asked Catherine.

"Sure," said Madeline. Her stomach lurched as she added, "That's where Emily's wedding dress is."

She was about to lead the two other girls out of her room when Vicky asked, "What's that?"

Madeline turned, wondering if perhaps the ghost of Emily Simms had left something else behind, something she hadn't noticed before. So she was surprised to find Vicky pointing to the dolls lined up neatly on the bookshelves.

"That's my foreign doll collection," Madeline replied.

"Can I see it?" Vicky had already crossed the room. She knelt down in front of the shelves. "My goodness! Where did you get so many dolls?"

"My uncle, mostly," said Madeline. "He travels all over the world and he started the collection for me."

"Look at that one!" Catherine went over to get a closer look at a Japanese doll. "What a beautiful dress!"

"It's called a kimono," Madeline explained.

"My uncle brought her back from Japan when I was six."

"What about this one? Can I pick her up?" Catherine pointed to a Victorian doll.

"Sure. She came from England."

Catherine pointed to a wooden Native American doll. "Did he bring you this one, too?"

"No, that was a birthday present from my mother."

Madeline was relieved that her friends had forgotten about going up to the attic. She went over to the shelf and sat on the floor between Vicky and Catherine. "Every one of these dolls has a story."

"Oh, tell us!" cried Catherine. "I want to hear all about them!"

As Madeline took the English doll down off the shelf, she thought about how strange this visit was turning out. She'd expected that Catherine and Vicky were there because they were interested in the ghost. Yet it was turning out that they were more interested in *her*, and the dolls she'd collected over the years.

"This doll," said Madeline, stroking the English doll's hair, "is the one that started my whole collection... "

IT'S IN THE ATTIC

She never finished her sentence. From up in the attic came a crash, followed by the shattering of glass. Madeline and her friends froze as a blood-curdling shriek cut through the whole house.

8

"What on earth was that?" Vicky asked, wide-eyed.

Madeline didn't answer. She was too busy scrambling to her feet and heading toward the door. If her hunch was correct, the thing responsible for the terrible noise wasn't from "earth" at all.

"Do you think it was the ghost?" Catherine turned white.

"You said you wanted to see her," Vicky reminded her in a soft voice.

"I—I thought I did." Catherine swallowed hard. "But now—"

"I'm going upstairs," Madeline told them.

"We'll come, too," Vicky said quickly. She stood up, holding out her hand toward Catherine, who'd stayed glued to the floor. "Maybe we'll get to see Emily Simms!"

Madeline didn't wait. She was already dashing up the stairs, toward the attic.

Blood rushed through her temples as she neared the top step. The late afternoon sun was low in the sky, casting just enough light into the attic to see what made the crashing noise. The old mirror was lying face down on the floor. Pieces of broken glass were everywhere.

Something else was torn to pieces, as well. Something white. In the dim light, Madeline saw that Emily Simms' wedding dress had been ripped into shreds.

"What happened?" cried Vicky, running up the stairs behind her.

"Is it the ghost?" Catherine demanded. "Is it Emily?"

Madeline didn't answer. She sensed a terrible presence in the attic. It was Emily, she knew. And she could feel her anger.

"Emily?" she said gently. "Emily, are you here?"

A low voice cried out from deep in the shadows. "Get them out!" it cried. "There's no room for intruders here!"

"It's her!" Vicky whispered. "It's the ghost!"

"They don't belong here!" the voice wailed.

It's in the Attic

"*You* belong here! Come with me!"

"She wants you!" Vicky cried out in a voice filled with fear.

"I think she's jealous of us!" Catherine added. "She wants you to herself."

"Mad-e-line! *Mad-e-line!*" The sound of the ghost's wavering voice calling her name nearly made Madeline faint with terror. "I need you! I don't want to be alone!"

"She knows your name!" Catherine was so frightened she could barely get her words out.

Madeline stood frozen to the spot. It was almost as if she'd come under a magic spell. She knew she should run. Yet the ghost was too hard to resist. Her powers were so strong!

Suddenly the sound of someone bounding up the stairs behind her snapped her out of her dreamy state. She turned and saw her brother hurrying toward her.

He glanced up at the broken mirror and the torn wedding dress, and saw the terrified looks on Vicky and Catherine's faces. He grabbed Madeline's shoulders.

"Get out of here, Maddy!" he cried. "You've got to get away!"

"No!" Madeline insisted. "I have to stay. This

is where I belong!"

"Run, Maddy! Get away while you can!"

Her desire to stay with Emily, to help ease her pain, was almost overwhelming. But somehow, some part of her heard the urgency in Brian's voice and believed he was right. After hesitating only a moment longer, Madeline turned away. Her feet were so heavy she could hardly move them as she started down the stairs.

"That's it, Maddy," he said gently. "Come on, you can do it."

She couldn't remember making her way down the stairs. The next thing she knew, she was sobbing, her face pressed against her brother's shoulder as he hugged her tightly.

"There you go," he said in a soothing voice. "Good for you, Maddy. You did it!"

"I'm getting out of here!" cried Catherine. "I've never been so scared in my life!"

Vicky wasn't far behind. "This house really is haunted! I'm never setting foot inside again!"

When the two of them left, Brian sat down in his room with his sister.

"She's dangerous," he said seriously. "Emily Simms is after you, Madeline. She must have picked up on the fact that you're kind and sympathetic. Somehow she's come to believe that you can make her feel better about the terrible loss that she never got over when she was alive—or even after."

Madeline nodded. "She's taking me over, Brian. She's starting to control me." She bit her lip. "I'm scared."

"We have to find a way to stop her, Maddy." Brian looked at her. "And we have to do it before it's too late."

9

That night, Madeline lay awake for a long time. She was desperate to find a way to release the tortured soul in the attic. And not only to free Emily Simms, but also to rid herself of the ghost's threat. She tossed and turned, trying to think of a solution.

She didn't want her family to do what the Wilsons had done—run away. Lying in the dark, Madeline realized for the first time since she'd moved that she didn't want to leave this house. She'd already grown attached to her new life. Just as her mother had said, new things only seemed new for a while. She'd already started thinking of the big old Victorian as her home and Fulton as her home town. She was starting to feel that she could truly belong here.

As for Emily, Madeline knew that the reason she still walked the earth was that she'd never gotten over her broken heart. She was still waiting for Charles, hoping to find out what really happened on what was supposed to have been her wedding day.

Suddenly an idea clicked in her head. She sat upright, knocking her pillow onto the floor. Perhaps there was a way to help the ghost of Emily Simms find peace, after all. Maybe, just maybe...

The next morning, she was actually humming as she sat down at breakfast. Brian glanced up from his bowl of cereal.

"What's up?" he asked, relieved to see her no longer shaky after the previous day's scare.

"I think I know a way we can help Emily Simms rest," she whispered excitedly. "If my plan works, she'll finally find the peace she's been searching for—and so will I."

Brian looked at her in surprise. "What's your idea, Maddy?"

It's in the Attic

"I'm not going to tell you, at least, not yet. First I want to find out if it's going to work. But if it does..."

Madeline didn't dare finish her sentence. She was hoping too desperately that a few hours of playing detective would help her find what she needed: the answer to the question that had caused Emily Simms so much heartache.

The Fulton Public Library was nearly empty late that October afternoon. Madeline was glad. She was going to need help finding what she'd come for—if it existed.

She headed for the research librarian's desk.

"Is there something I can help you with?" the young woman asked as Madeline stood shyly in front of her.

Madeline nodded. "I don't know my way around this library very well," she said. "I just moved to Fulton a few days ago."

"Then this is a good time to start learning." The librarian smiled. "My name is Ms. James. What can I help you with?"

Madeline realized how nervous she was as she explained what she was looking for. She was afraid she wouldn't be able to find it. And if that were the case, she didn't know *what* she would do.

She was relieved when Ms. James finally nodded. "I think I can help you," she said. "Come with me."

Please let me find what I need, Madeline was thinking as she walked toward the library's microfilm machines.

She had thought that meeting a ghost was frightening. Yet, her mouth dry and her heart pounding wildly, Madeline realized that the possibility of losing the one hope she had for freeing Emily's soul was a hundred times worse!

10

It was nearly dark by the time Madeline rushed home from the library. She ran nearly every step of the way. The biting air of the chilly night made her wrap her thin jacket around herself more tightly. Yet even that didn't keep her from shivering.

Tucked in her pocket was a copy of a newspaper article from a local paper in a town way over on the other side of the state. The issue of the

It's in the Attic

Tylerville *Star*, where the original article had appeared, was almost a hundred years old.

She'd found what she'd been looking for. Yes! Madeline's eyes had grown wide as the librarian had shown her the viewing screen. At last she'd found out the truth about Charles Day.

Now, she had to find out if it would do what she hoped it would.

As she neared her house, she thought how scary it looked. The sun had gone down, and a dark, unfriendly autumn night covered the town. Only a few lights were on in the house, making the windows on the lower floors glow. They looked almost evil. The other windows were dark, like hollow, unseeing eyes.

The bare trees cast odd shadows on the outside walls of the house. They looked like long, knobby fingers. Madeline looked up into the sky, hoping to see stars. Instead she saw only the full moon, pale and round in the black sky.

The heavy wooden front door creaked as she pushed it open. She stood at the bottom of the staircase for a moment, listening. Her mother was in the kitchen, getting dinner ready. Brian was in the living room, watching television. It was too early for her father to be home.

Madeline took a deep breath. The time was right. Ready or not, she had to go ahead.

She climbed the stairs slowly, growing more and more fearful with each step she took. She hoped she was doing the right thing.

The stairs creaked loudly as she made her way higher and higher, up toward the attic. Her palms were wet and her stomach was in knots. She knew she had to do this, but she was still afraid. She didn't know if her plan would work. All she had was hope—the hope that she'd finally stumbled on what Emily needed.

Standing in the attic, her hands shaking, she lit the candle. She jumped when a circle of spooky shadows sprang up all over the room.

Yet her fear passed quickly. She knew she had to concentrate on what she was about to do.

"Emily," Madeline said softly, standing in the middle of the attic. In one hand she held the candle. In the other she held the piece of paper from the library. She glanced at it in the flickering light. The letters were so small she could hardly make them out.

Yet she knew exactly what they said. At the library she'd read them over and over to understand what they told about the past.

"Emily," she called again, this time more loudly. "Emily, are you here?"

Cold air suddenly swept into the room. Madeline felt something soft brush against her. She let out a sharp cry.

Part of her wanted to run away. Her heart was pounding so hard she was afraid it might burst.

Yet she knew she had to stay.

"Emily," she said firmly, taking a step forward, "you must listen. The words I'm going to read to you are from a newspaper printed on your wedding day. The date is June 21, 1901."

She paused, running her tongue over her dry lips. She knew that Emily was not only there with her, but that she was listening. She was almost certain she could hear Emily's heart beating.

"Yesterday," Madeline read in a loud, clear voice, "in Tylerville, twenty-two year old Charles Day was run over by a horse-drawn buggy. The police reported that he was killed instantly. The young man was crossing the street, heading toward Stone's jewelry store, when he was hit from behind."

Madeline paused. Tears streamed down her cheeks. "You see, Emily, Charles didn't come to your wedding because that morning he was killed in a horrible accident. His family should have told you what happened, but they didn't. They probably wanted you to think he'd changed his mind about marrying you."

The attic began to feel strange, as if the air were growing fresher, as if the heaviness were lifting. Madeline could feel the air slowly moving upward.

"Go to him, Emily!" Madeline cried, a catch in her throat. She wiped away her tears. "Charles does love you! He always has! He's waiting for you on the Other Side. You must go to him.

"Find your happiness, Emily! Find your peace! Hurry to the man who loved you, the man who'll love you for the rest of time!"

Suddenly the attic window flew open. Madeline was so startled that she dropped the newspaper article. The flame on the candle blew out. She stood in the dark, alone.

Yet Madeline wasn't afraid. As the window opened, a fresh breeze blew in. The stale air that had filled the attic only moments before was completely gone. Instead, it was as if she were standing in an ordinary room in an ordinary house.

A feeling of triumph rose up inside her. Her

plan had worked! The ghost of Emily Simms had been set free. The woman with the broken heart had finally found peace.

Heading down the stairs, Madeline thought about all the things that had happened to her this week. She was beginning to settle into her new life here in Fulton. She was making new friends, getting used to her new school, feeling at home in her new room. Her old life was starting to feel very far away.

She realized that she couldn't be like Emily. She didn't want to waste time holding onto the sadness of what she'd had to leave behind. She too had to move on. Taking hold of whatever life offered her was a little bit frightening, but it was also exciting. In fact, it was as much of an adventure as having a ghost living in her house.

She went into her room, wanting to be alone.

Something caught her eye the instant she stepped through the doorway.

The writing in the dust on the trunk had changed. There, in the same handwriting, were the words, "Thank you."

Madeline was about to reach down and touch them when she heard her brother come bounding up the stairs.

FRIGHT TIME

"*There* you are," he cried. "Mom wants us to help with dinner. She's been looking for you everywhere."

"I was up in the attic."

Brian folded his arms across his chest. "Were you visiting with Emily again?"

Madeline shook her head. "Emily's gone."

Brian looked startled. "She's gone? Are you sure?"

"Yes," she said. "She's with Charles. Emily Simms is finally where she's always belonged."

From downstairs came the sound of a telephone ringing.

"Mad-dy!" Mrs. Johnson called up the stairs. "It's for you! Catherine wants to know if you'd like to come over to play with Vicky at her house."

"Got to go," Madeline told her brother breathlessly, heading down the hall.

"Busy social life, huh?" Brian was grinning. "I guess you've got no more time for ghosts."

"That's right," Madeline called back, glancing at him over her shoulder. With a smile, she added, "Right now I've got other things to do!"

192

Made in the USA
Middletown, DE
27 October 2016